MW01598357

Pottersfield Press

The Governor
of
Prince Edward Island

Rick Bowers

Pottersfield Press

Canadian Cataloguing in Publication Data

Bowers, Rick
  The governor of Prince Edward Island

ISBN 0-919001-31-9

I. Title.

PS8553.084G68   1986   C813   '.54   C86-093847-5
PR9199.3.B68G68   1986

Published with the assistance of the Canada Council.

Book Design: Lesley Choyce

Cover: "The Window" by Aré Gjesdal, Devil's Island, c/o 2154 Shore Road, Eastern Passage, Nova Scotia B0J 1L0 Canada

Pottersfield Press
RR #2, Porters Lake
Nova Scotia, Canada

Contents

The Return Man

Technically, John Leo MacDonald was not a return man like the others. He hadn't done any fighting over there, had no military ribbons. He didn't get a veteran's pension, was never seen in a legionaire's beret. There were people who didn't think he was a return man at all. But he had spent four years of his youth in Germany. He left for war but found it finished when he got there. Some said that he was the luckiest man alive, to have landed in Europe just when the peace was struck. Others seemed to think it all the worse for John Leo — he had missed the action, but still had to face the results.

He returned to Lot Point, P.E.I. in the late fall of 1949. Everyone was surprised to see him. John Leo had never let on when he'd be coming home. He never wrote. Had never gotten into the habit of it, he said. He wore a civilian shirt tucked sloppily into army pants, as he sauntered down the lane. Like everyone who returns home, his face smiled while his eyes searched. He had hitch-hiked up from the train station in Summerside; was too impatient to wait for the evening bus to take him home. There was nothing to do in Summerside but watch people walk by and listen to bullshit. It stood in the way of his return, he said.

John Leo was out working the thresher with the other fellows early next morning. He worked steadily, concentrating on the sheaves as he fed them into the roaring mouth of the machine. But there was a wide space around him, the space that a return traveller lets others enter only as he speaks about where he has been. During smoke breaks, and breakfasts, and late evenings outside, before the chill of nighttime sent everyone home and up to their beds, some of John Leo's doings overseas came to be known. He was part of a large group of Canadian and British soldiers that were stationed in the heart of the Black Forest in Germany. They searched the woods for land mines and dead bodies. John Leo talked about how the bomb squads used to burn out enemy bunkers, pump them full of water, and then blow them up. They used to collect small arms fire and contraband explosives, and set them off at the end of every week for fireworks. Then there were the "stiffs," as they were called. They were the bodies of boys usually, destroyed by weaponry and ruined by the very soil that their childish patriotism sought to defend. John Leo said that the filthy rotten smell of them was something he could never get out of his head. Where practical, the remains were identified and buried in the main garden area of the closest village. It was John Leo's job to dig the graves.

All in all it wasn't that bad over there, John Leo insisted. He figured he had learned more than he ever could in any schoolroom at least. By the time the bodies got to him, they'd be wrapped up. He said that those with name tags were almost always called "Wolf," or "Wolfie," or something like that. Seemed to be the most common name over there. Every now and then a desire to open the shrouds and take a look would come over him. But he never did. Sometimes, looking at those narrow dead bundles, he could hardly stand it; would feel a sickening heat in his throat and around the sweatband of his cap. But he'd keep on digging, pretending he was digging for clams on the beach back home, or remembering the time he helped mix cement for the foundation of the gospel hall out at the corner.

The place where John Leo spent most of the time was a beautiful town called Baden-Baden. He thought there was a Canadian Air Force base there now. Anyway, he said the town was spread out more than most of the little villages of the Black Forest — the "Schwarzwald," as they called it over there. It wasn't hard to picture what it must have looked like before the war, with its large green lawns, lovely downtown parks full of shrubs and bushes, and the warm springs that were supposed to be so healthy for the teeth and bowels. John Leo described the houses of Baden as large and white, with red rooftiles and little iron gates out at the front. Some places had fared better than others. There were cobblestone streets too. But the big tanks had torn up a lot of them, and most of the individual stones had been bulldozed into a large pile that just about covered the fountain in the center of the town.

On his days off, he helped a couple of old German women who were trying to replace a vineyard that had been burnt out when the allied troops marched through. He heard that some of the best wines in the world came from Germany. When he wasn't digging graves, he ditched rows on a hill sloping up to end at a castle that covered the top. The place was off-limits to service personnel, but John Leo loved to look at it. It was so high up and fancy-looking, that he thought it must have bore some resemblance to the castle of Heaven in the scriptures. Crouched over, setting sprouted twigs in the little holes he had made, he used to look up at the massive structure and think of the bread, and the wine, and the many mansions. The name of the castle was "Schloss" — at least that's what the old women told him. That was about all they ever said to him.

John Leo said that the hell of it all over there was that no one would talk to anybody. Nobody could be trusted. All the old women wore black, and moved their shuffling feet with a determination one didn't dare to interrupt. The old German men, too, maintained stony silence as they sat on benches or stood by the pile of rocks downtown. They would congregate in the afternoons like a bunch of aged hoodlums, with their large mustaches, knobby canes, and deep angry wrinkles. Their silent observings projected a type of hate that was all the more terrible for being a promise that they were too old to act upon. They were all that remained; the young German men were gone. The only young men left were fellows like John Leo — imposters, foreigners, functionaries left behind by conquerors. They were endured with silent anguish. John Leo said he always felt guilty over there, as if he were being blamed for some horrible thing he hadn't done.

But John Leo never thought about things like conquest or occupation. That was politics. He was just a stranger in a strange land. And Germany was a Christian country just like Canada or Britain, he said. There were good and bad Germans just like there were good and bad Englishmen, good and bad Canadians. All people were the same deep down. He dug graves, felt shame, did what he was told, and took off his cap whenever he saw the old German priest. Anytime any of the local children strayed near him in their curiosity, John Leo always held out buttons, or chocolate, or bits of cloth. They'd snatch them and run. Run from a grave-digger, run from a fool, thought John Leo to himself. There were some older girls too — some not that old — who bargained with the soldiers for all they could get: rations, medicines, cigarettes. They got whatever they wanted, as long as they gave up what was wanted — what groups of armed men have always wanted from the women of men destroyed. John Leo said it still made him feel rotten to think of it. It wasn't right to take advantage of the misfortune of those people. It was indecent. But, over there, that's what "climbing the language barrier" was all about. And there were some fellows, John Leo said, who like to brag about doing a lot of "climbing."

Anyway, John Leo would lean back in his chair, take a deep thoughtful breath as he remembered Baden, close his eyes, and relax in the familiar clutter of his mother's old kitchen. He was given eight weeks leave that fall after he came home. He said he was a "free man" until after the new year. But everything reminded him of Germany. When he went with his father to pick out the Christmas goose over at Kelly's, he told them about the time some fellows plucked and roasted a swan for Christmas dinner over in Baden. He could never get into a game of cards without talking about the German deck he had traded for over there, with the face cards so ancient and queer-looking that they seemed evil or magic. Every time he went by the gospel hall out at the corner, he'd mention the old bombed-out church that he and the other Canadians were housed in. He said that it almost made a fellow dizzy to look up at the height of the curved ceilings. The gospel hall at Lot Point looked like some kind of bungalow; but, from any part of Baden-Baden, the huge church there looked like a castle with its pinpointed spires rising up into the sky. John Leo used to joke about how he had come down in the world, about how he had lived in a castle vineyard and been a gravedigger for German knights killed in battle, but had returned to his former occupation as just another shitforker in Lot Point, P.E.I.

For the first little while after his return, people were always dropping by to hear about what things were like over there. There were return men too, like Harvey Jelley and old Wilson, who had seen action in the Black Forest — old Wilson had been there in the first war. John Leo told them he had left everything in good hands, as he opened packages of cakes and squares left at the house for him by some of the local women. The women often noted how thin he looked. John Leo would only laugh and say that if he could just find a good woman for himself he would soon fatten up. He would think of Anna Jeffries when he joked that way. He heard that she was married now and living over in Halifax. But he would think of another Anna too — one he never talked about — the one in Baden-Baden whom he used to walk with on the vineyard slopes. She was a little older — seemed older than she likely was — and had two little children, a boy and a girl. John Leo was never quite sure if both children were hers, or if one belonged to someone else. Families were so mixed up over there after the war, that everyone seemed to be on their own. Anna never explained anything. She always looked as if she were crying, and John Leo never knew if it was her sad face or her sad situation that drew him to her. Often, they walked together in secure parts of the forest out past Schloss. Sometimes, she let him hold her hand. But they never spoke much. Neither knew the other's language. Never "climbed" that barrier either, John Leo would think with bittersweet satisfaction. There was something pure about walking with Anna, something that didn't require language. It struck John Leo that perhaps people spoke too much most of the time.

After he had been back home a few days, things started to quiet down. There weren't as many visitors, and John Leo liked to get out of the house, liked to take long walks nowhere by himself. His walks usually took him to the old clam cove around the far end of Lot Point. He was told that a couple of the neighbor boys had drowned down there one summer while he was away. It was an empty, sandy, breezy place where the beach grass rustled in whispers and time was easily lost. He stood facing the wind and watched the first snowfall of the season that year blow in off the water. He started off counting every flake he saw. They disappeared into the water one by one, and were gone forever. Then he shut his eyes tight to lose count, to let the number of snowflakes no longer matter. John Leo told himself that nothing mattered, that he was not to blame, that he should forget everything he ever knew.

But the old cove where he stood, looking out at the gulf with its punctuations of red sandbars and jagged whitecaps, brought back things to John Leo that he could never forget. It was here that he and Anna Jeffries used to meet in the evenings. No one ever saw them as they laid in the tall grass, trusting each other's nakedness as children will. Everything was a clumsy, fleshy secret to them. The wind hissed and whispered "yes, yes" through the grass. He knew he loved her then. John Leo had a job that summer, digging clams and tarring dorries. He was fifteen years old, making twenty cents a day, and had already been out of school three years. The raw breeze bit him now, as he looked back at the uneven trail of footprints he had left on the beach. The high tide would cover them forever. In this very cove, he and Anna swore to love each other forever, and to get married someday. He wondered which of the three had given out first: Anna, him, or the vow of love they had made.

The harvest had been taken in early with John Leo home to help. It was a good thing too, because the snow came to stay shortly after. John Leo joked that both he and the snow were home for the season. Winter was his favorite time of year; the air at its freshest. He couldn't think of anywhere in the world he'd rather be than home. He was singing carols to himself three weeks before Christmas arrived, and would always have a lengthy discussion with Mr. Morrison after service on Sunday mornings. He told him about the old German priest — Herr Peter was his name — over in Baden, about how part of the church that he was bunked in over there was set off for masses and private prayers. There was always someone there — no matter what time of day or night — heads bowed, whispering over their beads. Old Peter was always there too, speaking softly with a light lilt to his voice as if he were singing. It was Latin, John Leo thought, and it seemed to grace the interior of the aged cathedral with power and importance. John Leo would listen quietly from a distance, look at the huge empty spaces between the columns that held up the roof, and at the gaping holes in the walls of the church where many of the windows had been shattered. They were holes of war — like the holes he dug each day. One night it struck him that in the day the holes let in the light, and in the night they let in the darkness. The thought of it was overpowering, he said, and his eyes filled with tears as he spoke. Reverend Morrison put his arm around John Leo's shoulder. They sat together in silence the rest of that forenoon, and no one went back inside the gospel hall until after John Leo had left.

A few evenings before Christmas, John Leo built a windbreak out of snow, and lit a fire of driftwood and alder bushes down on the beach. He poured kerosene on his uniform and watched the fabric burst with flame when it hit the pyre. He threw his German playing cards into the flames as well, and marveled for a moment at how each ancient face wrinkled into blackness. The fire burned down to an ugly charred ash, its smoke like a burnt offering or the stench of final sacrifice. John Leo doused it with snow. It cooled down to a hopeless mush. He felt the empty triumph of his own assertion. Shovel in hand, he thought of the vineyards of Baden-Baden, and consoled himself with the thought that he had probably planted two or more sets for every grave he had dug.

He figured things were more than even. He had done his part. He went to work for Hiram Shaw, grading potatoes through the rest of that winter. He crouched in the basement shadows of the hanging lantern and bagged spuds all day. Blowing on his chilled and aching fingers, he would say that he never wanted to be a soldier in the first place. It was just something to do at the time. He had claimed to be eighteen when he really wasn't, had taken the oath when he was too young to know what in hell the words meant. Besides, the fellows who had made it to combat were automatically released at war's end. And they were heroes too. For John Leo there was no getting out so easily. He was a volunteer. But now that he was twenty, he no longer wanted to live by the decision that a sixteen year old had made. He wasn't even sure any more if he was the same person who had wanted to join the army. Hiram Shaw told him there was nothing to worry about, told him to stay quiet. Nothing would be said.

That Christmas was a nervy one around the house and throughout the community. There was a secret in the air that wasn't really a secret at all. John Leo had only been out to the gospel hall a few times since his return, and then had given up going altogether. So when Mr. Morrison asked for prayers to be said for a confused and worried member of the congregation, it was generally understood to be John Leo whom he was talking about. Of course some members of the congregation said that the preacher could have meant any one of them. But the next spring found John Leo still around Lot Point, still working for Hiram Shaw, still talking about his army days in Baden to anyone who visited the house. There were those who figured John Leo had skipped out on the army, and thought he had done the right thing. Others said nothing, and their silence breathed condemnation. But Lot Point is a tightly knit little place, and John Leo was one of its own. He was kin, and was to be cared for regardless — like the blood relative one defends before even the closest of acquaintances, regardless of how unworthy that relative may be.

The army came looking for John Leo a couple of times through the spring and early summer. He always seemed to know when they'd be coming, though, and stayed over at Hiram Shaw's or spent a week with his Uncle Jonas who lived on the old dock road. Military Police from over in Gagetown, looking bored and a little offended, asked around about John Leo, but nobody ever let on anything. When questioned, his parents said they hadn't seen John Leo since back in 1945, when he went to train for the army and was sent overseas. After a few further visits — once by an army Captain — they received a letter about John Leo from Ottawa, but put it in the stove without showing it to him. For John Leo's part, he insisted that the military should be happy to be rid of him. To the army, he was never anything more than "a useless 'bye' from P.E.I.," he said. They handed him a shovel and said "dig"; that was all. The day they took the shovel from him, he figured their contract was done. He had forgotten about the army, he said, and if the army could just forget about him they'd be even.

People look back down the tunnel of their own history, forgetting the side corridors that lead off to petty triumph, misfortune, regret. The present tense of possibility is always brighter than, if inferior to, former glory. John Leo, however, had never felt glory in anything except a distant vineyard in Germany, and a bombed-out old cathedral in which he used to sleep. He could forget the army, he said, but could never forget his memories. Even though his stories of Baden-Baden grew slightly repetitious over the years, he felt inside that he was always giving a fresh account of a lovely German girl who had held his hand, of her little children with their sad, dirty faces, of a time that was strange and holy to him. He remembered their walks, the view from the hills of the Black Forest, and Anna's silent, withdrawn strength. He thought of the little pleasures that take away part of the heart at first, before taking away life itself. Sometimes he felt as if he had missed it all, as if he should have stayed over there.

Memories are the places people live when they are adults. But the present insists on drawing attention to itself, the way a sixteen year old wears newly-discovered individuality — like a silly badge. Every teenager around Lot Point knew that John Leo had joined the army when he was only sixteen or so. But John Leo would always caution any of the young fellows who were thinking of joining the service. He would tell them that the army was all right if a fellow couldn't find anything better to do. Mostly, he would give the following two pieces of advice: a young fellow should stay in school as long as he had brains enough that the school would keep him; and, get married to a good woman young, or forget about them altogether and go to Hell on your own.

Then another thing happened that changed the outlook for any young fellow seeking a career in the Canadian military: the army, navy, and air force all joined together as one. It was done in the name of efficiency, but the forces themselves were not all that pleased about it. According to the papers, it was all a part of some larger identity problem. R.C.A.F. Summerside had its name changed to "C.F.B. Summerside." The return men were especially displeased, and they kept on saying it was just another way to get the word "Royal" out of sight so that there would be no more monarchy in Canada. No one seemed to be in favor of it but, once the government had gotten its way, disgust with unification toned down to simple ridicule about a uni-formed branch of the civil service.

John Leo heard about it on the radio — about the Canadian Forces Reorganization Act, and about the Armed Forces Unification Act — but none of it meant anything to him. It was like news from a place he'd never been. It distanced him even further from his former army days. Still, in a curious way, he always figured he was happiest back then — always enough to eat, always a bit of money in his pocket. And he felt as if he had helped people too, had seen a few things that made him a little calmer about all the craziness going on in the world. Year to year he got on the land in springtime, harvested gladly in the fall, and cut brush or fished eels through the winter. Often, he thought that somewhere, someplace — maybe beyond the stars of a black summer night — he was still in Germany, still walking with Anna through the vineyards, or still looking up from his army bunk at the vaulted ceilings of the cathedral while prayers were being whispered. His memories and his routines became interchangeable and unchanged.

But, for the Armed Forces, unification changed a great deal. Reciprocity of information between the three "elements," as they were now called, became the rule rather than the exception. Army intelli-gence at camps like Gagetown linked up with Air Force intelligence at bases like Summerside in one common communications grid. They now shared things like defence concentration data, sovereignty reports, and routine reassessments of men missing and away without leave. All information was available at the push of a button. Changes more noticeable were apparent too: Air Force blue and Navy blue blended with Army khaki to cover the troops in a particularly aseptic shade of green. As well, the newly formed Military Police of all three elements were able to get rid of their old shore whistles, blue paddy wagons, and khaki jeeps. After unification, the Military Police drove shiny black Chevrolet station wagons.

It was a shiny black Chevrolet station wagon that pulled up alongside John Leo on the first day of August, 1969.

He said he could never forget that day. The sun had burnt off the morning's fog and the afternoon heat was beginning to buzz. He had salvaged an old oyster crate off the shore, and was walking up the Lot Point Road with nothing on his mind but lunchtime. When the car stopped beside him, John Leo thought it was a tourist looking for directions. Instead, a terse young military face riveted him where he stood.

"Nice day," said the MP by way of introduction.

"It sure is that," agreed John Leo.

The driver, on the other side of the car, peered out at him too. John Leo tried to moisten his mouth but couldn't.

"We're looking for a fellow who once lived around here," said the MP, as he consulted his clipboard, "a MacDonald."

He looked at John Leo and looked back at his clipboard. "Yeah," he said thoughtfully, "a John Lee—o Mac—Don—ald." He pronounced every syllable as if he were speaking a foreign language. "Do you know him?"

"MacDonald's a fairly common name around here," John Leo returned. He felt the band of his cap tighten around his temples.

"This is the guy," said the MP, handing John Leo the clipboard.

John Leo looked at the photograph of his clean-shaven young face of more than twenty years before. Looking up again, his eyes met the MP's without a glimmer of recognition. He could see his own aged image in the pupils of the young man's eyes.

"Don't know him," John Leo said, as he handed the clipboard back. His hand was shaking and his voice sounded dry as a whisper but, in his heart, he really felt as if he wasn't lying.

Taking in a deep and stabilizing breath, John Leo pointed up the road. "There's MacDonalds live on up ahead," he said. "They could likely tell you more than I could. The place is just past a big clump of alder bushes on your left, about a mile ahead." He gave them the proper directions to his father's house. They'd hear the same old story.

John Leo always said he figured he hadn't shaved for a few days, and his hair had gotten greyer year by year as he crawled on to the forty mark. But he couldn't believe the look of his own face in the eyes of that MP. He said he looked like an ancient and worried king in the deck of

German playing cards he used to have. One thing was for sure: he said that he felt like an old man from that moment on.

"What's your name?" asked the MP, as the car pulled away.

"MacLeod!" John Leo shouted back — his mother's name before she was married.

He stood by the side of the road and watched the car go around the corner that headed toward Lot Point. He shut his eyes and felt the painful relief of the hunted, before moving his feet down into the ditch and across through the woods on the other side. He said that those young recruits likely saw his name on some old list in the guardhouse, checked the address, and decided to drive up from Summerside for the want of something better to do.

John Leo chucked the crate he was carrying into a bush where he could find it later, and came out of the woods by a field of Hiram Shaw's. He went around the field, passed the gospel hall, and followed a footpath back of the line road toward the safe familiarity of his Uncle Jonas' house. He slowed up and walked calmly down the lane.

Stopping here and there to pick blueberries, John Leo felt the afternoon sun on the back of his neck. He thought about the vineyards of Baden and about the best wine in the world. He knew it was something that he would never taste. For some reason he wondered if Anna was married now, if she'd had any more children, if she still walked in the hills around Baden. Anna Jeffries — he thought of her too — married; no doubt she had plenty of kids. John Leo suddenly realized to himself that he would have been married by now too, if he hadn't dug so many graves. For a second it all seemed so clear to him. He felt as if he were part of something forgotten and far away from which he would always be returning. He would never be able to stop. At the same time he remembered, almost without thinking, that it was his fortieth birthday.

Yesterday and Forever

The evening of the afternoon we put him in the ground, we all met at the Horse's Coach Tavern. "He'd have been here tonight," piped Wally Hines, flushed and a little teary. One look at the shape Wally was in meant we all had a little catching up to do. "Leave two apiece," someone ordered.

Keith set the cold ones all around. Everyone fumbled for money, but he held up both palms to stop the effort. "I'll keep it all on a tab, boys," he said. It settled us down like a benediction. Keith knew the importance of things like strong drink and eternity.

He had died Friday night. "Couldn't hold it on the road around Jude's Corner," said Len Gillis, shaking his head. We all agreed it was a bad corner. "Probably they should put up some lights around there or a bit of guardrail," he suggested.

"I can't understand it," said Tim Walker, motioning in the general direction of Jude's Corner, "He must've driven that road a thousand times." He took a long drink, nodded in assent to his own point and continued, "Of course we all have, no one's perfect."

We all agreed that we all knew the road and that no one was perfect.

Amid the chatter more beer came around. Keith set them up briskly. "Hard to believe, though, isn't it," he commented.

"I still can't believe he's gone," said Wally Hines.

Len Gillis agreed, "I was in at the wake last night and again this afternoon before the service, and I still can't believe it. Everyone sitting around with long faces, his sisters crying, and him looking like he was going to jump out of the casket any minute, flinging cushions and cut flowers like it was all a big joke."

We all laughed at the thought of it. Laughed hard and drank, and laughed more. "He'd be the one for it," someone squeaked, and we all tore into it again. It all seemed incredibly and refreshingly funny. The rush settled down in declining spasms.

"But he is gone, sure enough," Len Gillis said thoughtfully.

"Yes, and it's not good to stare at a dead body anyway, for fear of the mind playing tricks. I guess old Rachel Shaw tried to get right in the coffin with her husband the other year in at the funeral home. She was certain she saw him start breathing again."

"When you're gone, you're gone."

"Yes, and he's dead enough," continued Tim Walker. "If you'd have been there Friday night when they took him in, you'd have believed it damned quick. I guess he had a big hole in his neck just under the one ear. There was nothing they could do."

"I heard he was dead before the ambulance even left the hospital."

Conversation split up as a new round of beer arrived. Along with the drinks arrived Blair Hennessey and Jimmie Williams. "Drinking 'er up big, boys?"

"Got to keep it flowing."

Everyone settled in, pleased at the new company. We had a broader base to pile memories. Some cigarettes were lit and stories flowed:

"Remember the time he turned eighteen," began Tim Walker, "He and I turned eighteen within a week of each other that summer."

"You mean you can remember it?"

"It's a wonder—the way we boozed it up that weekend. Swilling the rum into us like it would save our souls, and his poor old dad telling us about how, when he turned eighteen, he was in Italy."

"The poor old bastard."

"Yes, a few drinks and he'd be right back there in wartime."

"Thank Jesus we never had to face it."

"Ah well, he's together with his father tonight," said Hennessey. He drained a cold one, long and tasty.

"If it was one of us gone, he'd have been here tonight for us too," Wally Hines bleared, his chin cupped in hand.

"That's what it's all about," Len Gillis agreed. "Remember that time in Halifax? That big beer garden at the Armories there?"

"Jesus, what a piss-up that was," laughed Hennessey, covering his face.

"And him drunk as a two-toed boot telling that cop about how we were lost militiamen, and all the way from P.E.I."

"The way we were drinking, I'm damned sure we'd look it too," replied Tim Walker.

Uncontrollable laughter curled around and through us again. The shame of it had shuffled off that afternoon at the graveyard and it now united us ridiculously and completely. We indulged. The ensuing silence allowed us to drink quietly and privately for a moment. Hennessey called out for more beer.

Jimmie Williams emptied bottle into glass and nodded thoughtfully, "He was tight-lipped too. He could face it with his chin up. I remember that time at Hector Fielding's funeral. He told me: he said, 'I'd never want to go out like that, Jimmie. I'd never want to suffer through old age like that.' Those were his exact words."

"He got his wish," said Tim Walker wistfully.

"He and his grandfather were awful close," Len Gillis added.

"He would have never felt a thing. It would've been all over in a flash."

"He never suffered."

"We should all pray to be as lucky."

"I wish he was with us tonight," Wally Hines said, getting up from the table.

"Steady, boy, steady."

Keith slipped into Wally's empty seat. Plunking down a glass in front of him he winked, "Just tonic water, boys. Time for the bartender's break."

Talk went on about the tavern's business, about work, about money. But the accident, the funeral, and memories of him while he was living filled the grey space of our table fuller than present realities, the cigarette smoke, the soft light from behind the bar.

"Goldie felt bad she couldn't make it to the funeral today," Keith observed. "Just getting back last month off the maternity leave, she didn't have enough hours saved up to take off. I wouldn't doubt she cared for him more than half the old birds that were there."

Goldie MacAuley filled in for Keith behind the bar. She was a fleshy blonde. Had been out with him just two nights before the accident. There was an awkward silence as Goldie set beer all around. She had a long sad smile.

"Women really don't have much say in it, do they?" Tim Walker said, after Goldie had collected the empties. "It's like they bring us into the world, but it's up to us to take ourselves out of it."

"I don't know as I'd care for either job."

"No," Keith agreed ruefully, "Sometimes it's tough to face, isn't it? He was a damned fine guy, though. Had my sister out a couple of times in high school."

"What! and you trusted him?"

"I'd sooner trust him living than any of you devils dead," laughed Keith, headed back to the bar.

"Ah well, we'll be dead a long time after we're gone, so let's act alive while we're living," Hennessey intoned, glass aloft.

"Here's to life, be it over tonight or tomorrow!"

The beer flowed down us all at once. We were connected in one fluid motion. Nothing mattered but the flow of talk, of memory. Time seemed enclosed by the parameters of our table. It was harnessed by every yesterday we'd had together.

Len Gillis set down his glass, empty. "Remember that night drinking out back of the Protestant graveyard?"

"I was never so sick in my life."

"Wasn't that the night of the grade ten graduation?"

"Yes," Len chuckled, "and he kept going on about how it wasn't right to be drinking around a graveyard like that. Said it lacked respect."

"Didn't stop him getting as drunk as the rest of us."

"Christ yes, and now he's in there forever."

"You two clowns came tearing in through the bushes screaming like a pair of banshees."

"I was never so scared in my life."

Jimmie Williams came back from the bathroom. "Jesus, boys," he chuckled, "I think Wally's down for the night. I think he's passed out in the cubicle."

"He'll be all right."

"How's he getting home?"

"I'll see how he's doing when I lock up," said Keith assuredly.

"Wasn't that the time he spent the night in the drunk tank?" Len Gillis continued. "Jesus, he must have been in poor shape."

"No doubt he'd be in pretty raw shape."

"Don't know how in hell he got separated from us."

"He must have been pretty well out of it though. I mean if you can even tell them your address, they'll at least drive you home."

"Time flows when you're having rum!"

"Jesus Christ! and I'm supposed to be in Charlottetown tomorrow morning at eight o'clock sharp," Tim Walker exclaimed, looking at his watch. "Someone's got to keep the economy going," he joked.

"Don't spend it before you bite it!" Len Gillis hollered after him out the door, adding quietly, "Don't know what the hell Tim's hurry is. It's tomorrow already."

Hennessey was still at the bar talking with Goldie, and Jimmie Williams went to check on Wally. "He'll be all right," Keith insisted.

Through mingled "goodnights" from bathroom and bar, Len Gillis and I entered out into the damp summernight air. We stood in the middle of Central Street and looked down to the water. There was silence. Light off the tavern's front porch dispersed into the deserted street. We started home together.

Down at the waterline, the tide had gone out leaving an empty beach hard as pavement. It disappeared into the fog. Somewhere, behind the mist, water soothed and coaxed. It had a stabilizing effect. We stood silent, listening, looking out where the mist and water joined. It was as if we were receiving information, the darkness saying, "Look on and on and on — this is forever."

A night's drinking had passed into yesterday and there was nothing more to be done. The cool moist air washed our faces and parted us as if we'd finished a day's work. I became conscious of separate presences. We each had our own thoughts.

After some moments Len Gillis took a deep breath, "May as well head home," he said. "The mother'll be up frying ham soon enough. Be nice if she was up now, and me coming home sober as a judge. Might patch up relations a bit."

"I'm ready for a bit of a sleep myself," I answered.

"Got to keep going," Len assured, as he moved up the shore road on his way. "A fellow's got to keep moving or that's the end of him."

I could hear him chuckling into the mist. Then all was silence again. Last night's drinking seemed a week old already, and his funeral a lifetime away. It surprised me for a moment to realize that I couldn't fix an image of his face in my mind. Yet, in the darkness of an empty shoreline it scarcely mattered. Tomorrow would come with some people subtracted from the world, some people added. Its futility disgusted me. But I felt vaguely foolish as well — like in the forfeit of a game you were going to lose anyway.

Hands in my pockets out of the chill dampness, I strolled on up the beach. I clenched loose change in each fist and remembered settling up Wally's end of the tab. Seemed strange to think of it now. The vastness of night stretched out before me as incomprehensible as eternity, and as ugly as an open grave. I knew I'd stop off for a moment at Jude's Corner on my way home.

Shelfoon

The obituary referred to him as Augustus X. Shelfoon, but the full name in print was only a pretense of information. Those who cared to, simply called him Shelfoon. Place and date of burial were specified, but his surname was his only link. And no one in town could recall a time when he wasn't there. Regardless, people talked about how he had trained for the priesthood in Boston; how all the studying had made him crazy. Others believed that he had been gassed in the trenches during the Great War and never fully recovered his mind. Yet Shelfoon was never at mass, never in any Remembrance Day ceremonies. In fact he was rarely seen outside. He ran a store down by the harbor. On that, everyone agreed.

Behind the counter of his little kingdom he was at once fragile and monolithic — a wrinkled little man dwarfed by years of gravity. He sat immovably hunched over, his large speckled hands clutched in a permanent attitude of prayer. Shoulders, bunched under an over-sized shirt, were strapped together by large police suspenders and supported a sharp, never-quite-shaven chin. He looked like a captive, his withered old face blankly shriveled into the center of a toothless, munching mouth. A flabby nose hung out between eyes that were brokenly sunken and unblinking. His stare was effortless and void. He always looked the same.

Rocking slightly on a hard-backed chair, he gazed endlessly at a large oval picture of Christ. Holy, over-gorgeous Eastmancolor robes of light/bright blue surrounded a golden figure with flowing auburn hair and a sacred fire-engine heart. A multitude of yellowed envelopes and post cards — some supposed to have come from as far as the Orient — were tucked in behind the icon which dominated every feature of the enormously overpacked and disorganized little store. It covered the entire wall like a miracle occurrence. And Shelfoon cringed continually on the other side of the room behind the penny candies, muttering in whispers, "I never sleeps. I won't sleep. I thinks of our Savior and I never sleeps."

Directly behind where Shelfoon sat, a naked light bulb burned. Day and night it burned in tune with an old, crackling beamascope tube radio. Together they provided a continual background static, a hum that gave the room its only sense of reality. The monotone was like a chant, a source of power. But neither appliance did much to brighten the dim little interior. One small grimy window provided negligible light through sallow cellophane as it competed pointlessly for attention with the sacred heart of Jesus on the other wall. It was a place of endless empty shades.

Sitting there in his own silence, Shelfoon disinterestedly presided over an assembly of weird and lost subjects. He was centered in the cartoon-like surroundings of outdated calendars with their perversely animated puppies and kittens; busty, redlipped Coca-Cola girls on swings; a heroic sailor framed in a lifebuoy, ready-aye-ready with Player's; the highland lass leaping miles high over Export "A"; the Sun-Maid raisin girl vainly offering sustenance. The advertisements carried on out the door where some ancient election posters and old newspaper filled chinks in the shingled sides of the unpainted walls. On the door frame an Irving polar bear thermometer had given up registering the temperature at ten below zero, Fahrenheit.

The roof of the old place sagged as if the whole thing was about to fold in the middle and disappear into the ground. It had always looked that way. Scattered wrappers and ragged grass surrounded the tiny structure as it leaned against the abandoned cable slips where the ice boats used to dock years before. Only the wharf rats still hung around down there, hissing through the spring nights till the heat of summer drove them back under the planking.

It was said that Shelfoon used to feed the dirty things, and that was how he'd come to be missing a couple fingers. But his hands were never unclasped long enough to really notice and, when they were, they moved so quickly and dexterously that they seemed to be marionette hands operated tirelessly from another world. The misshapen claws handled merchandise, tallied figures, and snatched payment with an impatient urgency that made it clear the customer was an inconvenience, an interruption. His existence was restricted to silent transaction, quiet dismissal, and renewed absorption in the crazily resplendent shrine across the room.

The huge picture hung in seeming opposition to the store's disorganized goods. Large mysterious puncheons crowded around the wall, supporting stacks of rain gear and other war surplus stuff like boots and wool socks and overcoats. The clothing gave off a faint buzz of diesel fuel and fish. Nearer the dimly lit counter, pine tar and must lent a stable browning aura to everything. Everything, that is, except the glowing object of veneration on the wall. And Shelfoon gazed endlessly upon it while shoestrings, jackknives, and hickory twist shared grubby counterspace with bubblegum, licorice, and girlie air fresheners wrapped in plastic.

Mostly, he sold cigarettes and newspapers. In the winter he had eels, oysters, or bootleg rum if you wanted it. Shelfoon himself never seemed to touch the stuff, but it was often said that if you had all the liquor he had drunk in his lifetime poured into one place, you'd drown trying to swim out of it. Some said that he had nearly drowned years ago himself and was constantly giving thanks for being saved. Others said it was guilt for having drunk holy water. In any case, someone jokingly asked him one time if he *ever* ate or slept. Shelfoon just looked at him and said straight out: "I never sleeps. I just think of Jesus and never sleeps" — and that was all.

Of course one day he did sleep — if you could call it that. He was found by Timmy and Terry McCardle one Sunday morning before early mass. Still sitting up in his hard-backed chair, Shelfoon's eyes gawked across the room, his sunken lipless mouth opened impossibly wide and locked in the gaze of Christ.

The boys said it was the worst thing they ever saw. It was as if something huge and horrible had escaped from the old fellow's throat. Yet, strangely, nothing about the place was all that changed. The same silent suffering finality, for which he could never be understood, still wrapped Shelfoon in an earnest attitude of supplication. The smiling advertisements, outdated merchandise and uselessly lit store were as superfluous as always. Only the colors of Jesus had life. The undertaker admitted to a real embarrassment as he had to break every remaining finger to unlock the permanently praying hands.

Nearly everyone saw a strange religious lesson to be learned in all this and some, now that Shelfoon was gone, even saw him as a saintly figure. But appearances can be misjudged. Everyone has an emptiness to be filled with what others see as personality and refer to as experience. His was simply deeper and more fully self-justified. Perhaps, in an objective sense, he only partly existed.

I saw Shelfoon earlier that same morning the McCardle boys found him. It was well after midnight, but the correct hour is a blur to me now. Donnie Graham and I were just getting back from the May Day dance at the Legion in Charlottetown. We had whooped it up pretty well and were still giggling over the pint we'd finished off just this side of Kinkora on the 225 highway. Not a Mountie on the road. Good thing too, because in the shape we were in the breathalyzer wouldn't have stood a chance. We saw the light burning in Shelfoon's place and figured some pop and fresh smokes were needed before we headed home.

The night was sultry for the time of year — hot enough to silence the wharf rats and cool enough that the harbor didn't yet smell bad. But there was a suffocating pressure in the air, a tension that surrounded and bound us once inside the store. Something about the place demanded submission by darkness, allowing us only what it wanted to divulge: a weird buzz of radio and light; Shelfoon's incessant mumbling; Christ's crystalline aura shining larger and more brilliant than ever before. It loomed over us with a lurid, volcanic portentousness. The place was unbearable.

Shelfoon held pencil in knotted fist, his mouth moving with the figures as he tallied up the bill. His shoulder blades stuck out like cleavers, and Donnie and I exchanged significant glances. We both felt the strain — a sense of urgent demand, of dangerous incomprehensibility. I had the distinct feeling that nothing in the world existed anymore except for the dumpy clutter where we were now pinned. And Shelfoon held us there, his hands again clasped and his eyes digging us like an inquisitor.

"Your car's not running too good," he stated after an impossible pause. It was the first time I'd ever heard his speaking voice.

His eyes were opaque, his mouth cavernous as he slowly continued, giving each word a solid dispassionate weight. "I know when things are done . . . it's in the sound."

The statement bound reality with factual disinterest. There was no way to respond. A distant roaring filled the room and I realized that it was an implacable combination of my car parked outside and the electrical hum of the store. It would not stop. The sound had an ominous and obdurately eternal moan about it — something Shelfoon seemed to apprehend and wanted to indulge. He craned his crusty neck out toward the road. His mouth emitted a breath of decay and resignation.

My old Rambler needed a motor job worse than I needed a job to pay for it, but mentioning my dubious "pride and joy" was only a gambit — Shelfoon wanted to talk, wanted to converse. It was as if he needed to disburden something of crucial importance. His pathetic little face beseeched us to hear him, but we laughed it off as if he was making a joke. The shock of his voice riveted us in an ignorant hysterical flush, and we deserted him with a hastily awkward and stupidly goodhearted goodnight.

I'll always be ashamed of it. He had information and we wouldn't stay. But Shelfoon got in the final words, and they seemed to toll from the depths of a knowledge at once petulant and certain. As we stood dumbly in the doorway, he turned his face back to the figure of Jesus, his head shaking weakly in dismissal. "You young fellows," he scoffed, "if I was going to drag myself in at this hour of the day, I believe I'd have stayed out and made a night of it."

Holiday At Lorne Shaw's

Every year, following harvest, Lorne Shaw would get on the bottle with some of his friends, and his wife would leave to spend time with her people over near Moncton. She couldn't see the humor in it; thought it damned childish of him. But he was long past changing now. His autumn ritual had eased itself into a regular pattern over the years. Mild threats to sell the farm, followed by contemptuous lassitude throughout the Prince County Exhibition Days, would get fair hearing and final reconciliation in all-night games of crib, stories, argument, drink. Over the space of a day or two all his old chums would find their places around the kitchen table, get their elbows on the oilcloth, their tobacco out of their pockets. Kernan and Willard McNeill would be there, Lester Lynch, Bobby Connors. They'd bring their wrinkled boyish faces, yellowed teeth, plaid shirts, and mottled farmer's hands. The end of the season called them as if by instinct, as if their time of rest could be blazoned in the late-burning lamps of Lorne Shaw's chilly kitchen—oil heating was always next year away—before another P.E.I. winter settled in around them.

"It's the same damned thing year in and year out," muttered Lorne Shaw. "We've heard it all before: 'barns filled with plenty,' 'presses bursting with new wine,' 'the first fruits of increase' and all that. But what good is it to a fellow that gets laid up all winter with nothing coming in but bills?"

Kernan McNeill squinted in cigarette smoke as he shuffled cards. "Winter's not a fit time for anything but reading the newspaper and what bills come in the mail anyway," he offered.

"Get up in darkness . . . go to bed in darkness—to hell with it."

"*Now* you're talking."

Cards were dealt with the certainty of years. The drink on the table and the cards in their hands rested comfortably in their renewal as friends. It pleased them to move through the cycles together. From the muddied schoolyard to old Mrs. Tanton's punishing yardstick, from Elmer MacLeod's gravel pits to the fish cannery down in Summerside to King George's call overseas, they had always moved as a unit: the O'Leary Road boys. Both McNeills had married sisters of Lester Lynch, and Lorne Shaw and Lester were first cousins. They moved on a line together, as inseparable from their own fertile stretches along the road as the O'Leary Road itself was from winding its way down through St. Augustine's Corner out to the Templeton shore.

Lorne Shaw shook his head and returned his hand to the dealer. "Farming's a gamble that just cannot pay off today," he said. "It's sunup to sundown and then worry all night. And the little man like you or me is completely out of it. 'Get into it big or get to hell out'—that's the message for farmers today." He raised his glass to the invisible spirit of futility. "Why, I got paid more last year by the government to dump the most part of my crop, and yet half the children in the world are supposed to be starving."

"I think I read somewhere that there's children starving to death right here at home."

"Nothing can be done, because nothing's getting done," commented Lorne Shaw. "The unions have got everybody out on strike at one time or another so the economy can't go forward, and guys like us just sink deeper and deeper into the hole because the price of food is where it all starts in the first place."

"It starts there and it ends there."

"If we had any brains we'd have a union too," declared Lester Lynch. "Every ditch digger and bottle washer has got someone to speak up for him. It's only the farmer that tries to go it alone."

"Yeah, but there's risk to farming that you don't get with a regular wage," answered Kernan.

"There's good years and bad years," Willard added.

"More bad than good, if you ask me," said Lorne Shaw. "If we really had any brains we'd do like Bobby."

Bobby Connors had been uncharacteristically silent up to now. He nodded his head with a knowing look on his face, before hiding it behind a handful of rum. "If you fellows done like me," he said, "you'd be a damned sorry lot."

He was usually quick and cheerful about the deal he had struck with the Provincial Land Development Corporation. No more backbreaking bullshit for him: the government had bought up the whole Connors property, reserved Bobby — 'the last surviving heir,' as they called him — life interest in the house and lot, and turned the fields into community pasture. It was rumored that he could live like a king just off the interest of the selling price. And he was still years away from getting the pension. He lived alone.

Bobby stretched out a studied row of tobacco in his palm as he nudged his glass ahead on the table. "What the hell, let the government devils take 'er all if they want it," he said. "Sell off to the government, and go on a government holiday like me." He licksealed his cigarette in one motion, reached for his refilled glass, and tossed off his rum as if he were sealing the deal again.

"Well that's easier said than done," answered Willard after a pause.

"With a wife and family you've still got to make a go of it somehow."

"You're goddamned right you do," broke in Lorne Shaw. "But every horse's ass you see is out running the roads on some kind of holiday or other. You can't turn a page on the calendar but there's some new government holiday invented for the bankers or the office fellows to enjoy, while the fellow that really provides—the milk producer or the vegetable grower—works himself into the ground and then wonders why he's crippled up at the end of it."

"As if it wasn't spelled out clear enough in the mortgage," added Lester Lynch grimly.

"That's the hell of it," Lorne Shaw emphasized. "We actually pay for the privilege of putting ourselves in an early grave." Somewhat miffed at his own conclusion, he reached for the deck of cards, shook his head, took another drink, and added calmly, "That's why I take my own holiday every year about now."

"Kind of hard to enjoy it when the wife makes off for Moncton at the same time."

"Jesus no. That's the best part—with the family all grown up and gone. There's never a young one born that isn't an unexpected mouth to feed in the first place, and a pestiferous little backtalker going out the door the next."

"They grow up quick."

"Don't they."

"Makes you kind of wonder sometimes if they're worth the worry."

"They're just another risk," cut in Bobby Connors. "If there's an early grave in the dealings, we've got damned little to say about it. Children are as much a gamble as a healthy spring calf or potato blight in the back yard: you pray for the best. And even if nothing goes right, there's plenty of time to make up for it. That's what holidays are all about, isn't it? Making up for your mistakes."

Bobby left an awkward silence lingering around the table as he reached for more drink. Glances shot quickly about his hunched figure. They were nervous, questioning: what was strange about Bobby tonight? The bottle came around, and Lorne Shaw cleared his throat before speaking. "When I think of the mistakes gathered around this table," he began, "I can only thank heavens they're too ridiculous to be damnable."

The old boys blurted laughter and guffaws, as they wrestled for the bottle. Kernan tossed the deck in the air, and cards littered about the group as if they were crazy rectangular leaves. It was a confusion of relief. The mutuality of shared experience and understanding glittered through their aged faces as rum poured its cheer into every glass. Bobby, left to himself, was ignored with an unchallenging purity reserved for only the closest of friends. He, in turn, ignored them as his eyes wandered over the intricacies of the table's oilcloth design. He was somewhere else, his comments an interference, as Lester Lynch handled the bottle and Lorne Shaw led the two McNeills in a chorus of "Auld Lang Syne."

"I know it's usually sung on New Year's," said Lorne Shaw, passing a handkerchief over his face, "but these get-togethers with you boys are just like New Year's to me."

"A blessing to drink in good company anytime," declared Lester Lynch, rising to his feet with glass aloft.

"Who dares begrudge a once-a-year holiday?"

"If I could just get Nettie to move out for a couple days in the spring, we'd make it a biannual event," laughed Willard.

"Too late now," Lorne Shaw said. "You've got to get them hardened to it when they're young." His face was red with drink and delight.

Since they were standing anyway, Willard and Kernan decided to square off for a few jabs, while Lester Lynch followed the call of nature out through the entry door. The two fragile boxers were soon collapsing in a fatigued and brotherly dance. Laughing at their own exertion, they dragged their chairs back up to the table where Bobby, still rooted to his chair, picked scattered playing cards off of the kitchen floor. He gave each card a deliberate and thorough inspection.

"I guess Lester's never been the same since that weak turn last summer," Lorne Shaw began.

Willard, pushing off his partner's renewed attack, plopped down in his chair and nodded. "If it wasn't for the wife, he'd probably not even be here today."

Bobby Connors sat up with a grunt, and slapped what cards he had collected on the table. "Well, I count what few blessings I got," he said. "And I figure one of 'em's never having tied the knot."

"Not even with that Fraser girl you used to take driving?"

"God no. She's better off now wherever she is, than she ever would have been with me."

"I heard she was out west somewhere; married, with four kids."

"Magdalena Fraser," ruminated Lorne Shaw. "She was so damned horny I used to feel sorry for her."

"You never had to worry about it."

"What was there to worry about? Those were the days: young, and a bit of money in your pocket, and a woman in the front seat alongside you — just like you got the whole world by the arse. But by Jesus once you get through those twenties the time sure begins to fly, doesn't it?"

"I guess it does," agreed Willard. "I'm not sure anymore if I was ever twenty years old or not."

"It's just like I said before," Bobby Connors explained as he crushed a butt in the ashtray before him. "Everything's just a gamble, and we've got no say."

"Well I'd say a fellow who's sold out to the government for a big price has narrowed the odds to his advantage somewhat," returned Lorne Shaw.

"I suppose," answered Bobby. "Not that you'd know a hell of a lot about it."

Bobby's response swung through the kitchen like a blade. It stopped Lester in the doorway upon his return. The room hung silent.

Lester walked into the tension of Bobby's tightlipped reply, and saw Lorne Shaw twisting the top off a new bottle. Kernan rolled a cigarette, while Willard silently moved his lips as he counted the cards in the deck, glanced under his chair for those still missing. No one was connected.

Lester clapped a hand on Bobby's shoulder. "If I had your money, Bobby, I'd burn all mine," he quipped cheerfully as he returned to his place. "You're not still laying down the law are you?"

"Me? hell no. I'm just saying there's nothing that a fellow doesn't take a risk on. No matter what good you get or what good you do, there's always going to be some hidden part to it that's not so good."

Bobby's tone was empty, impartial. It knitted the atmosphere of the table together again. But his rheumy eyes merely stared into his glass as he spoke, brooding, testing; imploring the others to pursue, to encircle and take hold of the silences he left. He looked up, smiled lamely, and took another drink.

Lorne Shaw was direct. "I think you should climb down out of the loft and tell us exactly what's on your mind," he said.

"Look," Bobby returned sharply, "to hear you guys mouth off, you'd think you had a few clues. My God, you've got all the world's problems figured out and yet your heads are still up your asses."

"What in hell is your problem, Bobby?" demanded Lorne Shaw.

"That's just it — there are none. We're living aren't we? All of us old bastards are going to live long enough."

He slouched over the table, his eyes rimmed red. Bobby's measured breath meant there was more to come, more to explain. He reached for more rum, poured himself a thoughtful three fingers worth, and twisted the cap back on with grimace. His movements were cautious, his face wan.

The others waited.

"The way I see it," he began, "you fellows have all got what you might call family farms: wife, kids, lots of machinery. I was always in it pretty small: some fishing in the spring if I felt like it, a few drills of potatoes and turnips — just enough to get by for myself. No one bothered me and I never bothered no one else. You'd think a fellow my age would have learned to depend on a sure thing. But then there's nothing that stays on an even keel for long, is there?"

The men moved slightly, inclining forward to catch every word as if jurors about to hear testimony. Bobby picked at his fingernails and gazed at the ceiling. "I figure this holiday I'm on began here the other spring," he continued. "One morning, just before I sold out, some folks pulled into the yard: an older fellow and two kids, a boy and a girl. Couldn't have been older than fifteen or sixteen. I'd never seen any of them before. Anyway, they said they were from down the other side of Charlottetown, had seen my 'For Sale' ad in the *Guardian*, and wanted to have a look at the place.

"It was early in the morning, milking time. Seemed a funny time of the day for anyone to be out looking at property. In fact there was something funny about the whole thing: the older fellow alone in the front seat, driving, while the young ones were together in the back. They were all tired-looking and kind of nervy, like they were on dope or something. Anyway, I didn't see any harm in them looking around if they wanted to, so I just swung back the gate for them and kept on my way to the stable.

"I never heard the car go back out the whole time I was milking. Of course I was only milking two cows then. And while I was running the separator, I could see the entire laneway and yard out the buttery door — I watched, but they never returned. So after a dish of breakfast, I figured I'd just take a walk back and see what they were up to. You never know; I figured they might be hunting antiques and were skulking through my buildings or something. You can't trust anyone these days. But, over the first hill I could see the car parked by the edge of the far woods. They were just backing it around to leave by the time I got there.

"Well you wouldn't believe the look of panic on the old fellow's face when he saw me. Something was definitely wrong. I could see the girl crying in the back seat. The young fellow didn't look too damned happy either. He held her head against his jacket, and her hair hung all stringy and curly down his arm. But I never let on anything, just jumped in the front seat to ride back with them. Talked about how the rear line runs off angled between Freddy Gallant's place and mine, and about how the place had been granted to my grandfather by Commissioner's deed back before P.E.I. had even joined the Dominion of

Canada. They weren't too talkative though. The old boy nodded his head and made small talk all the way back to the yard, but the two young ones never said a word."

Bobby Connors finished off his drink and leaned back in his chair. He wiped his mouth with the back of his hand and laid both palms gently on the table. "They sure as hell weren't back there to look at property," he concluded. "At least not to buy any."

The others shifted where they sat, reached for glasses. Willard McNeill caught his breath forcefully. "What in Christ's name were they doing?"

Seemingly oblivious, Bobby Connors examined his hard and broken hands. He squeezed the tips of a couple chapped fingers, slowly leaned over the table, and looked straight into the eyes of each face in turn. "I figure they buried a little baby back there," he breathed.

"Merciful Jesus," responded Lester Lynch, "What makes you think they weren't burying a little puppy or some other pet like that?"

Bobby exhaled wearily, as if he had explained it a million times: "If they wanted to bury a dead dog or cat, they'd have asked me straight out. And I'd have let them too. But there was too much secrecy involved, too much shame, fear — you could see it in their faces; believe me, you could feel it. Either that poor girl had the baby back there, or they drove in with the body hid in the trunk of the car."

"For the love of Christ, Bobby," Lorne Shaw interrupted, "Wait just a minute. How do you know they buried anything back in your property? God only knows what they could have been doing. And if it was all that secret, you're probably better off not knowing about it anyway."

Willard agreed, shuffling the cards while Kernan filled glasses. Noisily clearing his throat, Lorne Shaw reached for his drink. Bobby Connors felt the heat of his rising gorge, and swallowed hard. "Better off alright," he echoed bitterly. "They buried something back there and I'm none the better off for it."

Pinching his eyes tight against the swimming uneasiness of the room, Bobby stared straight down at the tablecloth's miasma of intersecting colors. "I saw the mound about a week later," he continued, "just inside the woods from where the car had been parked. It was all split up and heaved, like the earth always is wherever you bury a dead animal or anything. But it wasn't the shape you'd expect of any four-footed creature, God damn it."

Bobby ran his hands through his hair and took a deep, calming breath. His face was ragged, cut by the shadows of poor light and cigarette haze. "There was some skulduggery done back there, believe me. I was nearly sick to my stomach just looking at it."

"And you never let it be known?"

"I figured it best to keep my mouth shut. None of it was any of my business — the less I knew, the better. Besides, the government owns the place now and I'm clear of it. Government holiday for me. But when I think of the carryings on of that day and the faces of those two young people, it's damned hard for me to enjoy it."

He rose unsteadily, slapped away Lester's helping hand.

"Take it easy, Bobby," Lorne said.

"What the hell for?" Bobby countered. "We're all on holiday here. You wouldn't want to spoil the 'fun', would you Lorne?"

His bitterness swelled him as he pawed his coat off the back of the chair. His throat ached with dry heat, and the figures before him wove interconnectedly, as if embodying the cramps of accusation that twisted him from inside.

"Anyway," Bobby continued, with an indignant swipe of his arm, "I'm finished story-telling for tonight too. You guys can complain about your wives, your harvest, or your lack of days off all you want. No matter what you say—you've never had it so good. But as far as I'm concerned that government holiday of mine that's supposed to be such a big deal is buried with the little being that's lying back in my woods."

He turned his back on a silence that was sad, sympathetic, and paralyzed. His empty chair rattled with the impact of the slamming door. Outside, the night air hit him like a punishment, as he stood in the middle of the O'Leary Road and looked back at the glowing windows of Lorne Shaw's house. He felt miles away already. Moving along the pavement's shoulder, he shone his flashlight into the black bushes of the ditch. The entanglement of growth was suffocating, the trickling drainage of water a tittering embarrassment. His head seethed with the pain of anguish and drink, and he curled his fists tight enough to crack. He had promised himself never to tell anyone.

Neighbors

Jimmy Arsenault and a couple of the Fred boys used to run rum along the north shore from Lot Point to Foxley River. They'd put out at night from the Black Banks and get the booze from French ships, anchored offshore where the government fellows couldn't touch them. This was during the Prohibition times and, according to the government, "P.E.I. was good and dry." But there was probably more liquor in the country back then, than there has ever been at any time since. Once the government took over the liquor business there was no more fun in it, no more adventure. It became a simple matter of rationing to any and all; and it was an inferior product at that. Drinking lost the buccaneer appeal it enjoyed when the rum-running ships plied the waves. They were mostly from St. Pierre and Miquelon—those little French islands off Newfoundland—and they ran their illicit cargo all the way from the Indies to the silent little dorries of P.E.I. that claimed their catch by night.

Once a month—sometimes not as often—Jimmy and the boys would put a week's work into the space of about two days. They had to work fast and without a word. What they were doing was a serious crime, although nobody but a few churchmen and politicians really thought of it that way. Besides, it was only for the sake of appearances. Whether or not a fellow got on the booze was up to no one but himself. Jimmy merely provided a service to anyone who was interested. He and the crew would scramble ashore below the hanging lantern at Kelly's or Waldo Beck's. They'd load the wagon waiting on the beach, and drive the wood roads through to Jimmy's place. There, they'd cut the liquor out of large hundred gallon puncheons. They'd be at it all night; and most of the next day too; and everyone along the shore would know that they were at it.

The only thing Jimmy had to worry about was the Mounties. But there weren't that many of them around in those days. Besides, Jimmy had the perfect scheme for handling anyone suspicious who came nosing around. He had built a fox pen right in the middle of the yard, and kept a ragged old red fox in there. He had managed to pilfer a registration certificate from somewhere, and had it up under glass at the road in order to show the fox's ranch-bred pedigree. Anybody who asked too many questions would get the full treatment: first Jimmy would show them the pedigree certificate, then—in the gravest whisper this side of Father Brendan's oratory—he would explain to the offenders that his fox was about to whelp any minute, and that it was a tremendously delicate time for any strangers to be around. The prize vixen would eat her pups at the slightest provocation. The financial loss would be incalculable. The only thing to do was to leave as quietly as possible.

He was a born actor, was Jimmy; had a way with words that seemed to get him out of any tight situation. He said that a fellow had to be able to think quick if he was going to make money and stay single. But it's a good thing the Mounties didn't check up on his doings all that often, or he'd have quickly run out of whelpings and whisperings for the sake of that old fox. Still, the Mounties—and the government fellows too, for that matter—were mostly from away, and they didn't know anything more about good rum or fox furs than they did about the law itself. The Mounties were generally nice young fellows though; gentlemanly in a way. Jimmy considered them to be the clear ticket for apprehending murderers and civilizing the land of the buffalo but, as far as he was concerned, they simply got in the way of business.

And it wasn't difficult to know when business was underway. Take a walk past Jimmy's at midday, and if the light over the doorway of the old shed was still burning—Jimmy's was the only place on the road with a windmill generator—you could be sure that he and the Fred boys would be inside working at the rum. There were other signs too. For a week before a new shipment was due, Jimmy would sit quietly in front of the bank in at O'Leary, and inquire after the health of various members of the local citizenry. Then there'd be no Jimmy to be seen for a day or two. All during the time he'd be gone, the Fred boys would tie up their fishing boat and drive loads up and down the O'Leary Road. To an untrained eye this might go unnoticed. But the loaded wagon would rattle and clank with a payload of empty cans under a canvas cover. Anyone who wished to have a full can need only to point out he had been speaking to Jimmy in at the bank on the previous day.

The customer could expect to receive a half-gallon tin of rarefied rum, direct from the West Indies via the old shed behind the fox pen at the far end of Jimmy Arsenault's yard. All the time Jimmy and the boys were working on a new shipment, the gate at the road would be shut tight and the light over the shed door would burn like a beacon against the greyed whitewash. Inside, the crew would work steadily at running rum off into separate cans. The cans with the four x's across the front would be cut with water and the other type, bearing the figure of a man's hand, would be cut with cold tea. As a result, the "hand" drink turned out to be a darker rum, and many fellows swore that it was stronger than the "four x" type. But it all came out of the one barrel, even though Jimmy never let on. One thing was sure though: you wouldn't want to drink it without some watering down. Jimmy said that the pure stuff would stain wood, lift warts, and make a preacher swear.

Jimmy's was the next-to-last place on the road to the Point. The last farm was owned by Walker Morrison, Jimmy's next-door neighbor. They were powerfully God-fearing, the Morrisons—all of them. Liquor was not a part of the divine plan, as far as they were concerned. But if they disapproved of Jimmy's business dealings, they nonetheless agreed that he was untrustworthy enough to be in the right line of work. And Walker Morrison—who had known Jimmy's old dad, Felix, when he was living—wasn't the least bit shy about letting Jimmy know it either. He was five or six years older than Jimmy and had spent his whole life as a witness to the younger boy's misbehaviour:

Jimmy was caught trapping rabbits out of season before his twelfth birthday; Father Brendan tried to make an altar boy out of him, but he broke into the rectory and got drunk on communion wine; another time, one Halloween, Jimmy let all the pigs out of the Morrison pen, and slipped them one-by-one inside the front door of the house. Old Mrs. Morrison nearly dropped dead of shock the next morning when she came down to the kitchen. After another episode, in which Jimmy was caught tying fish nets together, Walker Morrison went next door and asked him directly: "Don't you ever feel guilty about what you do?" he demanded. "Yes," Jimmy replied, "real guilty. But I was taking up so much time at confession over it, that Father Brendan finally gave me the last rites and said 'begone.' "

It seemed as though everyone in Lot Point had their favorite "Jimmy" story. There was the way he used to get right studious and couldn't tear himself away from the books when, like the other kids, he was let off school to help pick potatoes. Or the time years later when he came home from Halifax with a floozy who turned out to be married to an important lawyer over there. Every fresh offense confirmed Walker Morrison's low opinion; and when Jimmy returned Walker's scythe one day, with the blade twisted out of shape and badly pitted, Walker had stomped into his workshed, applied the whetstone, and refused to answer his wife's call to dinner until his murderous fury had passed.

Walker Morrison considered himself to be a sufferer in the first place, and Jimmy didn't help matters. Once, he called Jimmy a "conscienceless rogue" to his face, but Jimmy simply replied that if it was meant as a compliment then he was proud to be one. Walker's bad stomach came back for a week that time. Another time, when Jimmy was just a kid, he had stood in the sugar bushes at the edge of the woods and pelted Walker with crab apples as he attempted to plow the road field. The barrage kept up until, finally, Walker dropped plow, harness, and all, and crashed through the bushes to grab the little devil—who was about fourteen years old at the time—and give him a good hiding. Then, handing Jimmy the hickory switch he had used, they walked along the line fence together and planted the shoot at the road between their mailboxes. Walker had tears in his eyes as he described the incident later to old Felix, but the old fellow just shook his head and said that he had never been able to control the boy, that Jimmy should have gotten more good hidings when he was younger. The hickory grew tall and straight, and branched out over both farms; and Walker could never look at the tree without feeling a little ashamed.

Through time, Jimmy grew into quite a big shot— in his own mind at least. He was always on to some big deal that was going to make him rich. He still bragged about the load of poplar he had palmed off on the McDermott-Henderson Company, telling them that it was peeled "swamp spruce" and perfect for pulpwood or fine furniture. For a while he sold salves and liniments door-to-door, but there was no money to be made in that. Then he got hired on at the MacKay Fox Farm in Summerside—at that time it was the largest fox ranch in the world. Anyway, to hear Jimmy talk, you'd think he was running the place. But then a picture came out in the *Guardian* showing old MacKay handing over a thousand dollar fox pelt to a couple of London buyers. Jimmy was just barely noticeable in the background of the photograph. There was no doubt but that it was him, though, and it showed him forking herring and fresh tripe into one of the pens. A lovely job that! For a while people called him Jimmy Herring or Jimmy MacKay on account of being such a blowhard.

But Jimmy was a neighbor, and neighbors deserve polite endurance at the very least. In Jimmy's case, more than the usual endurance was often required. Walker Morrison, however, would tell himself that it was all a matter of living up to the trial, of standing steadfast in the face of adversity. Besides, Walker remembered well that after the old house had burnt down, Jimmy had followed Felix over every morning to help rebuild. They were the only neighbors outside the family who offered. It was a grievous job too. The old place had been the first Morrison homestead, and Walker's dad never felt comfortable in the new house. But ten-year-old Jimmy had kept up everyone's spirits. He carried in the mail and pumped dippers full of cold water for the men. The "men" included Walker who, by this time, was old enough to handle tools and help carry. Even he, in the first flush of adult importance, found amusement in Jimmy's running monologue about how the House of Commons in Ottawa and the "House of Morrisons" in Lot Point had both burnt down at the same time. There was no denying that Jimmy was a smart little rascal. For a fellow who never paid much attention to school, he could read the papers and funnies, and kept everyone up to date on what was happening in the world. Even now, he always had a story about some strange goings on in some foreign country Walker had never heard tell of, or about the *real* truth behind the scenes of political and business matters. They'd often chat it up in the morning at the road, after the mail had gone. Jimmy would always wear an easy smile along with necktie and checkered pants.

Once he got talking it was hard to get a word in edgewise, and Walker would think to himself that if Jimmy lived in the States he'd either be an auctioneer or a gangster.

Walker stood out at the gate on one of these typical mornings in midsummer. He checked the sky for storm clouds. Then he gazed over toward Jimmy's buildings. Jimmy hadn't been out to get the mail yet; in fact Walker hadn't seen him for almost a week. His eye caught the burning glare of the light bulb over the shed door, and his usual suspicions were confirmed. Walker Morrison just shook his head in sympathy and disgust, was privately pleased that he himself had never known the taste of liquor.

Just then, Jimmy emerged from the shed and walked over to the fox pen. He waved at Walker from across the yard and began feeding the old patch through the fox wire. Walker could hear Jimmy's voice as he talked to and fed the old animal. It was a shame, he thought, Jimmy always had time for that shaggy crippled-up beast, while old Felix had practically starved to death during one of Jimmy's many absences. Anytime there was work to be done, Jimmy would be gone to the billiard rooms in Summerside, or maybe to a bootlegger's there. As for the fox, Jimmy declared that having it around would make him a millionaire someday. Walker had been by when Jimmy trapped the thing by accident in a rabbit snare. The wire had nearly cut off one of its puppy forepaws, and it had walked on three legs ever since. Jimmy had raised it up just like a little dog, but its puppy days were long since over. It spent all its time now, when it wasn't feeding, spinning in a circle with its tail in its mouth. A cruel thing, thought Walker, to keep an animal cooped up so long. The fur was flea-bitten and sparse, with bald spots of mange around the ears and snout. And the fact that this aged specimen—ever liable to whelp when the authorities were near—was a male, only made Jimmy that much more pleased in his ability to deceive; an ability that seemed to come natural, as he waved at Walker again and did a little dance with the bucket he was carrying.

Walker Morrison waved back but couldn't help thinking what a silly-looking figure Jimmy made across the way, with his white shirt and red suspenders. He had always dressed as if he were at a picnic; said he had to look good to feel good. At least Jimmy would never be overlooked in a crowd. Walker shook his head and smiled. Jimmy was too busy for idle chatter today.

Walker was just about to climb through the fence and pump water for the cattle, when he noticed a dust cloud billowing toward him up the road. He could hear a motor too, and cars were not all that common on the Island back then. In fact the only people who drove cars in those days were fox ranchers, Dr. Champion in Alberton, and the Mounties. And this car was approaching fast. Walker heard the roar of the motor hollow out, as the car passed over the creek bridge and came around the curve at the Wilson place. Jimmy had heard it too. And Walker caught his breath in surprise as he saw Jimmy spring like a cat toward the shed; saw the door slam behind him.

The light over the shed door disappeared into itself. Walker was shocked by the abruptness of it all. He knew something was up, and he wished he was somewhere else. But there was no time to think. By the time the Mountie car had stopped at Jimmy Arsenault's gate, Walker Morrison was standing right there too.

The motor was shut off, and the car sat quietly for a moment as a wake of red dust rolled by. Walker looked leeward to get his face out of it. His eye settled on the hickory tree—it was still referred to as the hickory "switch"—and Walker thought of the line between his place and Jimmy's. He could feel his own heart knocking as the Mounties got out of the car and started toward where he stood. Walker clapped one hand on the gate latch, and held up the other as if he could stop a train.

"Hey!" said one of the Mounties sharply, "We've got to get in there."

Walker put on his darkest Sunday morning scowl, and apologized in a strong quiet voice: "I'm sorry," he said. "The owner's away, and I can't let anybody in." Then after a serious pause, during which he wondered if he knew right from wrong anymore, he added, "There's a fox about to whelp."

The Mounties frowned at each other, stood at the gate and looked in. They were tall fellows—both of them—and they flanked the short sturdy frame of Walker Morrison, who nervously scratched his head and resettled his cap. He felt hollow inside, thinking about how he had once told Jimmy that there was a place waiting for him at the Dorchester Penitentiary. Looking at these uniformed police, he felt sick at the thought of ever having said such a thing to his neighbor.

Walker took a deep breath, swallowed hard, and gestured toward the fox pen. "That's the good fur right there," he said in a measured whisper. The Mounties continued to look on in investigative silence. The fox chewed on its tail and stared back out at them with those beady terrified eyes that foxes always seem to have.

"She's registered," Walker heard himself say in the nervous silence. He felt his throat tighten like a slip knot. Then, in his best Jimmy Arsenault rasp, he added, "One wrong move now, and she'll not let the pups live."

The fox gave itself a little shake, scattering sawdust and feces, and Walker felt ridiculous as well as fearful. Finally one of the Mounties whispered back. "Is this Jimmy Felix Arsenault's place?" he asked.

"It sure is," Walker returned with a sigh of relief. Then, in a sincere hush, he added, "We can talk at my place."

Walker Morrison stood on the running board of the Mountie car, and directed the driver down the lane. With the wind in his face, his jacket billowing free in the breeze, he felt a little like Robin Hood or Jesse James. He smiled at the sky, and thought about Jimmy and the Fred boys crouching in fear back in the shed. He took a deep breath of air and felt a tiny bit of silliness creep into his heroism. He imagined Jimmy and the boys would be escaped halfway to Summerside by now, and he wondered if he shouldn't have turned them in when he had the chance.

Walker never forgot that particular day. Standing on the running board of the Mountie car was the first car ride he ever had. And later that same evening, after the Mounties had long been gone, Jimmy came over to the Morrison place for the first time in years. He was drunk and teary-eyed. He said that he had discovered what a precious thing it was in life to have good neighbors. He went on and on about it, shook Walker's hand four or five times, patted him on the back. No matter what was said, Jimmy always twisted the topic back to what a great fellow Walker was and about how he had always looked up to him. He kept up the praise until, finally, Walker had to ask him to go—the wife had long since gone to bed, and it was after midnight.

Dark Moon of August

Winter was on the mind of Donnie Ellis as he sat
in his bathrobe, beer in hand. His thick hairy legs were crossed at the
ankles, and he wiggled his toes obliviously. A morning game show on
T.V. flung colors and rude noises across the room at him, but he paid it
no attention. He was thinking about the cost of stove oil, about getting
some wood out before the cold weather hit, about running the snow
plow all winter if old Ramsay would just get elected. Most of all, he
thought about the baby in Mary's belly. That morning in bed, before
she left for work, Mary had guided his head down along the side of her
smooth swollen paunch, and he had felt the movement, the life inside
her. The baby was due any day now. There'd have to be good dry heat
in the house for a new baby.

Donnie finished his beer and lit a cigarette. He blew out smoke
along with a sigh, and rubbed his wet head in the towel around his
shoulders. He got up, and stretched, and looked out the window. The
fat globe of the moon was settled low in the sky. Donnie thought to
himself that it looked like a round grey hole, an escape hatch out of the

universe where he might actually find a job. He shook his head with a bit of a snort; only crazy people think of things like that, he told himself. Still, there were times when he wondered if he wasn't losing a few cogs.

He headed out to the porch for another beer. On his way, he wondered if Mary had thought of any more good names for the baby. The roar of the T.V. followed him to the entry, and he had to step over a litter of writhing pups to slide his empty into the grid while simultaneously pulling out another. He snapped off the top with the opener he was carrying, and his gaze met Lady's sad doggy eyes. "Good girl," he said, looking away quickly. He knew he'd have to put some of those pups to sleep. He wished he could win the lottery, so he could afford to keep them all.

He dragged his bare feet back to the living room, thought some more. At least Mary would still get paid for the whole time she was off to have the baby. How long? he wondered. A month? God, as long as she gets back on afterward. The colors of the T.V. screen rearranged themselves into shiny new cars, smiling women in funny suits, and money. Before long the fuel bills would start coming in. Donnie sucked air through his teeth in quiet contempt. He felt a little useless. He had missed the job driving the school bus last year, and his unemployment had run out in May. There was no call for drivers at the moss plant this year, no carpentry work to be had all summer. They had been living off Mary's pay alone. But he had gotten used to the routine of it. He usually stayed in bed till Mary left for work. Then he washed all the breakfast dishes, waited for the mail. Since she had the car there was no getting away, even if he particularly wanted to. And any neighbors who weren't working at least had enough stamps to draw on the unemployment and spend it in town. As long as he could get through the mornings, he was happy. The afternoon T.V. shows were better. Donnie yawned big and wide and teary. Nothing could be done in any case. He couldn't even get the morning rug out of his mouth this morning. He sloshed down some beer, gargled, slouched in the easy chair, stared at the T.V., felt useless again.

The time seemed to have piled up on him in its day-to-day motions. It was the end of August already. Kind of made Donnie feel as if there had been no summer at all. And now the whole fall and winter stretched out before him. But he'd be a father. He felt good about that. And yet being a father was just having a title, not a real job. Being a mother—now *that* was a job. He thought of Mary: large, uncomplaining, practical. She did all the work, and kept up the spirits for both of them. He took another pull on the bottle. God, women were good. Now if God were really good, old Ramsay would be elected tomorrow, it would snow the next day, and he'd be driving the snow plow like Uncle Wincie used to when Ramsay was the member before. But snow was still a long way away; so was the election. And yet he might be a father by next week. Donnie stared at the ceiling, watched light flicker over it as the T.V. burst with another winner.

He had gone to see old Ramsay two or three days after Uncle Wincie's funeral. He'd always voted right, and old Ramsay knew it too. He wore the new tie Mary had bought him for the funeral. But he felt a little self-conscious walking around in a suit. He figured that everyone who saw him thought that he was some kind of a crook. Besides, Ramsay's office was over top of the bank, and the bank manager was one fellow Donnie didn't want to see again if he could help it. Anyway, he slipped up the stairs quickly without looking in the bank window. Ramsay said that he was glad Donnie could make it. He was concerned; you had to give him that. He knew the family. Knew what it was like to be out of work too, he said. Promised Donnie that he would get the job running the snow plow, just like Uncle Wincie had: the whole Western Road from O'Leary to Inverness, and all the paved secondaries in between. It was a big job but he knew Donnie was the right man for it. They shook hands again, and old Ramsay said that all the younger generation of voters was going to support him, was going to heave those rascals out of Charlottetown and give the average man more say again. Well, at least old Ramsay always had plenty to say. Standing in the hall, he had passed on greetings to Mary as Donnie descended the stairs, asked about when the baby was due. He wasn't a bad old fellow, Donnie thought, had done up Uncle Wincie's will and all the family business.

Donnie rearranged his bathrobe and took another drink of beer. Jesus, I hope Ramsay gets in, he said to himself. He could just imagine a frosty morning at 4 a.m., and him grinding gears on that big yellow snow plow. His train of thought ended there, however, as a head-banging series of yelps and whimpers started him from where he sat.

He had been too engrossed to hear the car pull up, but he knew who it was almost immediately. The dogs did too, and they continued their barking clamor as Carl MacDonald's footsteps trod the stair. Donnie could hear Carl talking to the dogs as if they were kids playing house: "How's the Mommy? How's the Daddy? How's the good puppies?" There were yelps of response, and wagging tails banged against the wall. Finally, Carl's back appeared in the doorway, as he pushed his forceful admirers away. "Don't let any of those damned things in!" Donnie shouted from the living room.

Carl already had a beer in hand as he plunked himself down in the rocking chair across the room. He looked out the window and at the T.V. screen. Donnie exhaled and took a drink. He half expected Carl would make it over today. They both knew the job they had agreed on: Lady's pups had been sired by Carl's dog, so Donnie and he were going to do the job together on the first day that Carl couldn't get out with the boat. The T.V. blurted between them. Pointing his bottle at the set, Donnie said "Turn that damned thing off."

"You're in a rare mood," Carl observed, as the T.V. picture disappeared into a white dot.

Donnie nodded without saying a word.

Carl took a drink and went on lightly, "No fishing today, so I thought I'd bring Daddy over to have a last look at his family," he said.

"I should've had that bitch spayed."

"You can't blame Daddy for the way things have turned out," Carl said. "She's a fine-looking pooch."

Donnie smiled. "Looks like Daddy and I are in the same line of business these days," he said.

Carl nodded in agreement and took a long drink. "Did Mary go in yet?" he asked.

"Could be any day now. She's still working."

"You heard anything?"

Donnie just shook his head and crushed out his cigarette. He had long since given up feeling anything when asked about work. And old Ramsay had told him not to say anything. Besides, he had grown accustomed to the drab light of cloudy mornings and his chair by the living room couch. He had gotten so he didn't feel like doing much of anything—least of all doing away with a bunch of helpless puppies.

"Too windy for fishing today?" asked Donnie, after a pause that seemed awkwardly solemn.

"Yeah," Carl returned. "Those inshore swells are a devil on a day like today. Not enough to damage you but, . . . well, . . . just dangerous."

Donnie got up and stood by the window.

"Besides," Carl went on, "the moon isn't right. There's no amount of fish gets caught during this dark time of the moon—especially in August."

"It's a strange time," Donnie agreed. He looked at the outline in the sky where the moon had dissipated.

"A strange time indeed," Carl nodded. "Nature comes to a stop this time of the year; like it's getting ready to decide whether we'll have a fall, or go into winter right away."

"Summer's over," Donnie said. "After the dark moon of August is passed and the Gold Cup and Saucer has been run at the driving park, that's the end of it."

"I've heard that alders cut during the dark moon of August never grow back," Carl added.

"I never heard that one," said Donnie.

"There have been fellows who gave up drinking at this time of year who never craved liquor again."

Donnie raised his eyebrows, looked into his bottle. "Probably it's the right time to drown puppies too, is it?"

"I'm afraid so," said Carl.

God how I wish I didn't have to do this, thought Donnie to himself as he got dressed. But at least he was going to do something. He closed his eyes and felt the morning drone of the night before in his ears. For the price of a pint and twenty-four beers I could've afforded to take them to the vet, he thought. He balanced himself on one foot, and tied the shoelaces of the other. He could hear the dogs yipping and frisking; could hear Carl out there with them. This isn't right, he thought. He looked in the mirror. He was going to be a father; a giver of life, damn it. Could he be a killer too? He gritted his teeth and left without an answer.

Donnie stood in the doorway, watched Lady nursing quietly, her head cocked to one side, sleepy, uncurious. Carl crouched beside her, holding his own dog and patting Lady gently. He looked up at Donnie. "Isn't that a sight?" he said.

"Jesus, I don't know what I'm going to tell the neighbor kids," Donnie responded. "They've been over here cuddling those pups every morning for the last five days. I practically had to fight them to send them home today."

"There's nothing goes together like kids and puppies."

"Yes, and I had to promise them the puppies would be here when they got back."

"How many are you going to do?"

"God, I don't know. Have to keep a few of them I suppose."

Donnie peeled open a green garbage bag, and Carl took it as his signal to take the male dog out. Nine pups! thought Donnie to himself, as he watched the furry little organisms attack Lady's underside. Like worms, he thought, like little cannibals eating the life out of her, replacing her. And her with her warmth and her shelter knowing it, loving it. Donnie tried to discern the neighbor kids' favorites, as he watched his hand snap three of the smallest right off of the nipples they were attached to. He paused. Recklessly snatched up another. Forced it into the bag of whimpering oblivion. He checked again to make sure that the white-booted favorites were still there. He slipped out the door to the car.

Carl had the motor running, and they were off in a minute like a pair of robbers in a getaway car. "God, I hate doing this," said Donnie, looking over the back of the seat at the squirming green bag on the floor. But they were committed now. They couldn't turn back without feeling as ridiculous as guilty. Carl turned the car onto the road without saying a word.

The motor hummed through different keys as the car shifted gears. Donnie's head was full of other noises. What if somebody higher up decided that he and Mary shouldn't have a baby. Could they just come along and put a stop to it? He could see himself grabbing off those puppies again; heard the tiny squeaks and mindless whimpers from the back seat. But it's not the same, he said to himself. He was doing the little beasts a favor. They wouldn't feel a thing. Still, he felt it was more a matter of his convenience than his mercy. He looked out the side window and watched the bushes of the ditch flash by. He focused on nothing. It was all a blur. He'd have to make good and sure that he got Lady spayed after this.

Poor Lady, he thought. She was a good dog. A perfect dog for a baby to have as a pet. They could grow up together; real companionship. Good protection too, with Mary home alone lots of evenings. But he never expected nine pups to show up on the scene. It must be some kind of record. Lady was still pretty much of a pup herself. And yet she'd had nine pups. At least he had left her five of her litter. He tried not to think of it.

At the creek bridge, Donnie handed the bag to Carl. He exhaled in relief when Carl took it. He watched Carl slide a couple of rocks into the bag, poke holes in the plastic, and knot the top. Then he turned away and fished for a cigarette as he walked back to the car.

Carl disappeared under the bridge. He returned in a minute, and put the car in gear without saying a word. They hadn't stopped long enough to shut off the motor.

That afternoon, at the Horse's Coach in Summerside, they retraced the steps of the operation. They went over it again and again, as if to justify it, to exorcise it. They hunched over the table and seemed to form a protective circle. Donnie said that he felt like a criminal. They both agreed that it was as if someone was after them, as if they were hiding out in fear for their lives. Their acceptance and their concern grew with each re-telling—and with each beer.

Donnie took a long contemplative look around the tavern. It was quiet, unthreatening. He felt a catch in his chest, and approached the subject from a different angle. "You don't know what it was like, standing over that brood with bag in hand playing God," he said.

"Imagine how I felt actually tossing the bag in the drink," Carl returned.

"How does a fellow go about justifying this to the neighbor kids? or to the wife?" asked Donnie abstractly. "Of course there are still *some* puppies left; their favorites too, I made sure of that."

"I suppose the kids'll think that some of the puppies just didn't survive."

"Here's hoping."

"Look," Carl said, "There's fellows in Montreal or New York would knock off either one of us or Mary with the baby is her, and not feel the guilt we feel right now."

Donnie hadn't thought of that. He ordered another round.

All the way home, Donnie thought about winter. Thought about that big yellow snow plow. He wished he could just stroll over to the garage and look the machine over. But if Gerard Gallant saw him nosing around, he'd know something was up. Probably he knew anyway. If old Ramsay gets in, I wonder how they'll tell Gerard, he thought to himself. No doubt Ramsay had plenty of secretaries to handle that sort of stuff. Besides, Gerard would get the unemployment.

"What're you up to tomorrow?" Carl asked as he turned the car in the lane.

"Another day of nothing," Donnie returned. Then he added, "I don't imagine I'll be too popular a cock over all this."

There were no lights on in the house when the car pulled up to the yard. An early grey gloaming had aged itself into darkness. Donnie got out of the car and felt the chill of late summer on his bare arms. He didn't know whether to go in or not. The place was silent, and he asked Carl in for another beer.

Donnie tried not to look at Lady as he stepped over her and her pups. But he was certain he heard a little growl in the darkness. Don't blame you a bit girl, he thought to himself as he flicked on the light in the kitchen. The first thing he saw was a note fixed on the fridge door:

> *Mary went right to the hospital from work. Mother and son doing fine.*
>
> *Mom*

Donnie's face contorted, and he snapped the note in Carl's direction. They hugged, dug fingers into shoulders, and shook hands. Donnie felt joy in his neck and strength in his forearms, felt as if he could lift Carl over his head. He could hear congratulations; heard Carl say that he would wait for him out in the car.

Once he was alone, Donnie sat at the kitchen table and cried. He buried his face in his arms and cried hard without really knowing why. A boy! A son! He thought he should stop crying, but didn't know how. The tears kept coming. He could see a whole life ahead of him from birth to death. And him as father. He let the tears roll in joy and agony. As he washed his face, he thought about maybe phoning the hospital, but all he wanted to do was get to the hospital right away. He wanted to see Mary and the baby.

He swept through the porch, and started crying again as he kissed Lady and every one of her pups. He put one of the furry balls inside his jacket to take to the hospital with him, and vaulted the front steps in a leap. He could hear the radio playing as he reached the car door, and he was already thinking about cutting wood tomorrow. There'd have to be good dry heat in the house for a new baby.

Uncle Ray's Advice

The first morning of June walked through the screen door of McKellar's camping trailer and started kicking him in the head. McKellar lurched himself awake, tried to roll with the blows. Cold daylight poked itself in behind his eyes. Hugging each shoulder, crossarmed, he allowed himself only enough information so that his teeth didn't chatter through a bone-cracking yawn. Settling, he felt the cruel freshness and drab predictability of another day. He emerged. He watched his own feet cover the length of the driveway. He was thinking of coffee at his sister's place: Eva's. She always knew what to do.

He'd had the same dream again: the one about him and Uncle Ray aboard an old sailing ship. It was an explorer's vessel straight out of the history books, and he was first mate under Uncle Ray's command. But the ship was in trouble. High seas and raging winds tossed the little craft like a cork. She began taking on water. McKellar shouted commands, sent men to key stations, ordered the sails trimmed. Waves lashed the deck; sent spray clear up to the topmast. He couldn't hear his own voice in the fear and confusion. Uncle Ray, however, grasped his arm in steadfast confidence. As usual, he was just about to name safe harbor, when the storm grew too violent and McKellar awoke. Disappointment rattled in his head with the dry pain of another morning after. What port did Uncle Ray have in mind? McKellar wished he could go back to sleep and know.

It was the same dream that had sent McKellar home that spring. He had sailed up to Montreal with the Abegweit on what was supposed to be an eight-week refit. It was a horny old time. But the rest of the fellows came back with the boat. McKellar stayed on. He whooped it up for almost a year. Couldn't believe it when he found the Abegweit's berth at the Vickers wharf empty. Spent the last of his vacation pay in a topless place called the "O La La." That night he had the same dream as he snoozed under the stairwell of some big building. Hitch-hiked home in two days on an empty stomach, only to find his wife six months pregnant—and starting to show it too. Worse: the fellow who had gotten her that way had moved in with her. McKellar had to sleep in the tent trailer at the end of the driveway.

Of course Tina wasn't really his "wife." They had lived together some three or four years in the same place though. It pissed McKellar off just to think about it now—about the utter betrayal of it all. At first he thought of rounding up a few of the boys and taking the place back by force. They'd storm the house and reclaim it. Send her to hell back to Halifax along with the snotty little greaser who was in there with her. But then McKellar came to think that he had to take some of the blame for the way things had turned out: he never wrote, never phoned, drank more money than he ever sent back. For all Tina knew, he might have been murdered up there. But she had heard that he was very much alive, if not too well. Still, as far as McKellar was concerned, Tina was the only woman that *really* mattered. The only one that he could look at and feel the word "love" inside. The old sailors used to call it "having a long leash," thought McKellar to himself, as he stumbled up the steps to Eva's place.

He was surprised that he had made it all the way up the hill—the hill that translates itself into a red cliff of greeting to first-time tourists and returning failures alike. It says, "Welcome to P.E.I." McKellar looked back over the twisted lanes and assorted houses of the village, down to the docks, and beyond to the choppy whitecaps of Northumberland Strait. This was the view that had washed his boyhood dreams; the view he used to gaze on as he imagined life beyond the rim of even the hills of Nova Scotia across the way. The world was big—he knew that; knew too that he would sail every wave of it someday. He'd be a deep-water sailor like Columbus, or Admiral Nelson, or his Uncle Ray. Unfortunately, time had watered down his dreams. He turned sixteen having never traveled farther than Portland, Maine. Instead of sailing the seven seas, he began parking cars on the ferry between Borden and Cape Tormentine. Mostly, that's all he had done ever since.

Even as he thought of it, though, McKellar knew that being a deckhand on the Abegweit was now a *former* job of his. There'd be no hope of brother Cliff getting him back on again after this. A trip or two to the Detox Centre was one thing—extended voyages on company time was quite another. Seemed to be the first point Eva made when he got inside the house.

"You only turn up here when you want something," Eva said knowingly. She tightened the ties of her bathrobe, crossed her arms in older-sister fashion.

Her unwavering glare drilled a hole in the top of McKellar's bowed head. He stared at the black pool of coffee on the table below his chin; balanced a burning cigarette on the saucer.

"You're the last person in the world who should be looking for sympathy," Eva continued. "And what about Tina? what about her?— not that you'd care anyway, with your selfish little sprees at dry dock, in town, and over in Halifax. My God, she's practically lived a single life the whole time she's been tied up with you. The fellow she's in with now will treat her better than you ever did."

Eyes closed, head in hand, McKellar almost tended to agree.

"This last escapade was just the icing on the cake. And what do you do first thing you're back? Root your nose into the Curling Club bar as if you'd never left the place."

The kitchen door slammed and McKellar's head leaped at the same time. Curiously, the room seemed cooler with Eva gone. Allowed McKellar to think that he wasn't the only one to blame either.

He peered into his cup, examined the coffee grounds with vague qualmishness. Slowly, and with effort, the night before at the Curling Club came back to him. The darkness was interspersed with laughter, sweat, the spilling of drinks. He remembered describing Montreal from the CN rail station to the Forum, and every watering hole in between. He brought on another round with the story of a whore who issued condoms "for *your* protection." And he had cried about Tina too. Put his head right on Gord Kennedy's shoulder and cried to all about his "deepest personal feelings." Someone asked him if he'd been drinking with the preacher again. He knew he'd never live it down.

McKellar could hear Eva in the hallway, hurrying the kids off to school. She told them that Uncle Ray wasn't feeling well, said they could see him after school. McKellar still hadn't gotten used to being an uncle; told Eva that the kids should just call him "Ray." There was only one *real* Uncle Ray in the world. But the kids called him "Uncle Ray," as they hollered their goodbyes to him in exuberant vocal disunison. "G'bye kids," thought McKellar to himself through cupped hand, and wondered if he had actually spoken out loud.

"You're a disgrace Ray," Eva announced as she poured him another cup. "I suppose next thing, you'll be begging Cliff to get you back on at the boat."

"I don't know," McKellar returned weakly. "I thought first I'd go see Uncle Ray."

"Don't you dare!" Eva shot back. "Leave that poor old man alone. The last thing he needs is to see a reprobate like you." Eva paused for a moment, seemed a little alarmed at her own ferocity. "He's not himself anymore," she said. Then, almost as an afterthought, she added, "Clifford and I visit him first leave each month."

"The kids too?"

"They usually stay over at Cliff's mother's. They wouldn't understand. Besides, it would only be a negative influence on them. I read somewhere that children have got to be nurtured with positive images: Easter eggs, Baby Jesus, Bambi, . . . you know."

McKellar couldn't help thinking that Uncle Ray had been the most positive image in his own young life. For a second he grasped memory of the sound of his parents fighting; remembered how he would shut tight his eyes and pretend that his bed was a sleek trimaran; that he and Uncle Ray were sailing around the spit at Chelton Beach.

"I thought Uncle Ray might like to see me," McKellar said.

"Well he doesn't want to see you. He doesn't want to see anyone. And what's more, Clifford doesn't want to see you either. He's got problems enough of his own trying to run that boat, than to stop and pick you up every time you take a nose dive."

"Every time you take a nose dive"—McKellar listened to the sounds of the words echo in his head. They strung themselves together with Eva's help to make a meaningful accusatory sentence. But he felt his own sense of shame inside, and it had nothing to do with the cutting suspicions of his older sister or the I-told-you-so look on

Cliff's face every time he reported another failure. Eva had married Clifford Monteith, skipper of the M.V. Abegweit. Good for them. They had kids and cars, and Cliff was thinking of running for mayor next election—superb. McKellar, however, had always found what he wanted a little closer at hand. Missed it when he didn't have it. "Can I borrow a couple dollars?" he asked.

Elwin stood behind the bar. He wiped glasses, wiped the counter, rattled ice. There was a sturdy gentleness in his manner: the gentleness of daytime quiet in every late night bar. He listened abstractly and with patience to McKellar's complaints, waited for the day's deliveries: the liquor order, the grocery order, the mail. Finally Elwin broke in on McKellar's aggrieved enumerations. "Let's not get too self-pitying, Ray," he said. "I can just imagine the whore of a time you've been having up there in the big city."

"It wasn't that great," answered McKellar into his beer.

"Sounded pretty rich last night."

"I exaggerated," McKellar returned. He searched for his smokes. "Tina is the only woman in the world I've ever cared about. But wouldn't you know it? I'm gone for a few weeks, and she shacks right up with some son-of-a-bitch."

"Might have been a little longer than you think," Elwin offered. "It all evens out anyway: you had your fun up there, she had her fun back here. Besides, Neely's not that bad a fellow."

Neely. The name went through McKellar's temples like a nail. He didn't know any Neelys, but he knew right then that he hated anyone who bore the name. He could just imagine them: a family of sex perverts; or maybe a bunch of inbred morons. He snorted to himself, tilted the glass high up to his mouth. At the same time, he felt a little ashamed. He set down the emptied glass, and stared at the lace pattern left by the beer froth. He was powerless, cowed deeply inside by what he knew to be a feeling of loss. He ached. Tina.

The paper arrived. Elwin placed it on the bar, went about his business. McKellar was left to himself. He watched Elwin clear the tables off, removing last night's glee, last night's folly. McKellar remembered again his "deepest personal feelings," felt the heat behind his eyes. He shook his head, lit a cigarette.

The dim interior of the Curling Club wrapped itself around McKellar and held him like a sullen child. He could drink here, could cry here, could tell all the lies he wanted and laugh as loud as he pleased. Everyone understood, laughed back. But he was still on his own. McKellar stared into his face in the mirror behind the bar. Why did nothing ever go right? He opened his hand, saw the hand in the mirror open at the same instant. He exhaled long and emptily, scattered his sense of injury, waited for Elwin to come back to the bar.

"Do you know what my sister said to me this morning?" he demanded. Elwin set a tray of glasses and ashtrays on the counter, and McKellar went on: "She told me, no, *ordered* me not to go see my Uncle Ray—my own uncle."

Elwin poured a beer.

"Can you believe it?—my own uncle. And you know what else? She won't even take her own kids to see him. Says it's a bad influence on them for Christ's sakes."

"How's the old boy doing?"

"Still in the nursing home, I guess."

McKellar paused thoughtfully, crushed out a cigarette. "Word is he's not himself any more. Poor old beggar. Sometimes I have the damnedest dream about the old fellow. About me and him on board a sailing vessel."

"Be nice if he could chart a smooth course for you now," Elwin said.

"Wouldn't it," McKellar agreed. He paid for the beer, lit another cigarette.

Wasn't that what the dream was all about? About where he should go next? McKellar took a long thoughtful drink. He remembered the model of the Marco Polo that Uncle Ray had built for him—"the fastest clipper ship in the world in it's time," he told him. He remembered again how he used to pretend he was sailing with Uncle Ray: sailing away as his mother cried and his father crashed about in the kitchen, cursing. Last night's dream was a pointer. He wondered why he hadn't thought of it before. McKellar knew that dreams were often borne out in reality, going right back to Biblical times. And Uncle Ray had the answer, had the advice.

Wise advice. McKellar smiled quietly to himself. That's what he needed. The type of reassurance you get from dear old grandfathers and local country parsons with grown daughters. Both of McKellar's grandfathers were dead long before he arrived, though. And McKellar hadn't seen the inside of a church since Cliff and Eva got married. Of course there was that night he took Tina walking in the graveyard back of St. Luke's. But that didn't count. Was damned sacreligious anyway. Even at that, it seemed as though she kind of liked it—a real secret between them. Something different. Tina said that she loved him because he was something different. He told her the same thing. McKellar remembered too that when he and Tina finally moved in together, old Uncle Ray was the only one in the parish who didn't stop talking to them. The old fellow had been around. McKellar knew he could talk to his Uncle Ray.

Waiting in the lobby of the nursing home, McKellar felt a little indecent and kind of small. He wished he had been out to see his Uncle Ray before. He perched at the edge of a sagging chair, figured the place must be two or three miles from the Curling Club. And he had walked the whole distance. Had turned down Allie Rayner's offer of a free ride in his cab. He could see Gord Kennedy right there beside him in the front seat, smirking. God how they loved to torment. It'd be nothing but dirt. Robbie Gallant was no better: asked him about his "deepest personal feelings," outside McSherry's as he walked by, but McKellar just shook his fist and kept on going. Animals, he thought to himself. The bastards were incapable of pity.

In one way, McKellar wished he could just stroll right back out the power doors. The place made him nervous with all its bright lighting, bare walls, and glass. It had that hospital drug smell about it too. McKellar smoothed the oily wrinkles of his shirt. He zipped his jacket up again. Seemed like a long wait. But the nurse had called him a "significant other," and he felt kind of important about that; didn't mind waiting even if smoking wasn't allowed.

"I'm Ray McKellar," he said with a little laugh. "My uncle and I both have the same name."

The nurse crinkled her nose and nodded, put telephone to ear.

"He's my favorite uncle."

"The client will be wheeled in shortly," answered the nurse, covering the mouthpiece of the phone.

McKellar wished he had a drink.

It was a shame Uncle Ray had to stay in a place like this—he who had traveled the world. He had been to every port from Shanghai to Amsterdam. "Call in at any one of them," he once told his eight-year-old nephew, "present yourself as 'Ray McKellar,' and they'll either give you a medal or call the shore police."

McKellar grew up on Uncle Ray's stories about people and places so far away: about little yellow men the same height as boys with bad eyesight and ten-foot wives; about a statue in Greece so big that the ship sailed between its legs into harbor; about big fish that jumped right into the boat and gave themselves up when the crew was about to starve to death. He often felt that he had grown up a good deal, too, the night his father held him by the back of the neck, telling his crying mother to take the girl and leave, to go somewhere else. Eva was sobbing, and McKellar wet his pants in terror. But then Uncle Ray came into the kitchen, put his arm around McKellar's father. They sat at the table and talked. As his mother pushed him and Eva toward their bedroom, McKellar could remember seeing the backs of his father and uncle in the lamplight. Uncle Ray wore suspenders over his bare back and looked strong as a wrestler sitting beside the thin frame of McKellar's father. McKellar felt that he had been rescued from death. That he would now be able to grow up and see the world.

But McKellar never got clear of Borden. He buried father and mother in St. Luke's the same summer before he turned fourteen. Eva promised Uncle Ray that she would take care of her "little" brother; and he was gone again, shipped out of Boston or New York. McKellar was working at CN Marine the next time he saw his Uncle Ray. The old fellow declared that his sailing days were over, that he hoped his well-studied nephew would carry on the tradition. But McKellar said that he'd have never met Tina if he had gone to sea. Northumberland Strait was sea enough for him now, he said. Besides, with Uncle Ray home for good McKellar could hear about any part of the world he wanted.

And Uncle Ray had seen it all. He was a whiz at navigation and knew about a million card tricks. It was said that the IQ tests couldn't be used on him. As McKellar got older, the stories he heard about his Uncle Ray got juicier: he was supposed to have been hooked on dope in the Orient, took holy orders from some swami over there; he was said to have lived with a black woman in the Panama Canal Zone; nearly killed a man in Bristol, England. McKellar never had the nerve to ask Uncle Ray about any of these rumors. He just listened and dreamed. Used to pray silently in the darkness of his bedroom that God would keep Uncle Ray and protect him from drowning on the seas or being killed by headhunters with their deadly blow darts. Now and then a letter would arrive with foreign markings all over it, and McKellar would know that Uncle Ray was safe. He would look up his uncle's position on a set of nautical charts that had arrived in the mail for him on his seventh birthday.

"Wonder what ever became of those charts?" asked McKellar to himself, as he focused back on his immediate surroundings. He felt as if he'd been waiting quite a while; felt ignored, resented. These medical folks love their diseases but don't give a damn about people, he thought. But then he remembered Uncle Ray telling him one time how life is just learning how to wait. Ride an even keel, he said. Anger just speeds up time and wastes it. McKellar felt again the little grip of fear that grabbed him the first time Uncle Ray said it to him. Could still remember Uncle Ray holding up both palms as he said it. Each hand had an "x" tatooed on it, right in the middle of the palm. McKellar thought they represented a holy mystery. Once, after his retirement, Uncle Ray explained that while plenty of fellows he sailed with were practically covered in tatoos, he'd had only the two marks pricked in to remind him what a waste of time anger really was. Whenever I get mad, he said, I just stare into my palms, realize the time I'm wasting, and wait for the rage to pass. McKellar found himself staring into his own palms just thinking about it.

McKellar wondered where in the far reaches of this hospital Uncle Ray was. Wished he had a chart of the place. Probably they were waking the poor old fellow up, dressing him, telling him his nephew Ray was come to see him. McKellar felt cheap. Uncle Ray had started repeating himself shortly after he stopped sailing. He got forgetful too. Pretty near burnt the place down around them one night, smoking in bed. When Eva and Clifford were building the new place up on the hill, he started accusing people of trying to kill him. Told McKellar that he knew a family in Hong Kong who would kill anyone if the price was right. One night they found him wandering near the cliffs at Cape Traverse. He said he had seen a light that begged him to follow. Eva took him to see a specialist. Uncle Ray was put in the nursing home. Seemed a long time ago now.

McKellar waited, felt uneasy. He wondered what Eva would say if she knew he was out here. He remembered coming home from Halifax and being told that Uncle Ray had been put away. He called her every name in the book and Cliff pretty near took his head off. Sitting there now, McKellar wished that he had studied to be a doctor so that he could give Uncle Ray his full attention and fix him up. Maybe turn back the clock a little. If it were only that easy. He spent an evening one time drinking with Williams, the lawyer's clerk in Summerside, and he told McKellar that Uncle Ray was being cared for under "The Incompetent Persons Act." He said it sounded worse than it really was. All it did was allow Uncle Ray to make out his will to Eva during what the lawyers call "a lucid interval." She and Cliff paid special expenses and were declared Uncle Ray's primary heirs and assignees. Everything was done all legal. McKellar never said anything. He figured Eva would only do what was best. But sometimes he didn't trust her. Anyway, she and Cliff were welcome to anything they could get off the old fellow. McKellar just wanted to talk.

Two nurses wheeled Uncle Ray into the lobby area. They flanked him like a pair of votaries. In his wheelchair, his head and face maned with ragged grey hair, Uncle Ray looked like an Old Testament prophet; like Methuselah, thought McKellar to himself. He could see the nurses speaking to him, moving their mouths in smiling niceties. Saw Uncle Ray nodding wearily, fraily. McKellar moved forward, gritted his teeth with concern. He could hear the nurses talking now. They sounded as if they were speaking to a little boy, or to a belligerent drunk. Uncle Ray said nothing. McKellar hoped that he would be in one of his "intervals."

The nurses nodded in McKellar's direction and left him alone with his uncle. For a second McKellar wished they would have stayed. He wasn't sure what to say. "Been quite a while since I seen you, Uncle Ray," he said.

The old man made no response. He remained hunched over in his wheelchair, stared into the palms of his hands. McKellar noticed that he was strapped in across the chest.

Something was stinging inside McKellar's throat, as he drew his own chair closer. "How's the food?" he asked lightly.

Uncle Ray closed his eyes, turned his face away. His movements were ghostlike. McKellar felt as stupid as he was scared. He took hold of his uncle's shoulder, was amazed at how thin and bony it felt in the fabric of the hospital shirt. The old man looked where the hand rested on his shoulder, raised his eyes to meet McKellar's own. "What are you doing here boy?" he asked with a contemptuousness that McKellar had never heard before. It sliced him. He felt the heat and shame of boyish tears, as he heard himself respond: "Uncle Ray," he stammered, "where else should I go?"

McKellar watched his uncle as he formed his mouth into a little pink "o" beneath his beard. He shut his eyes, and his aged breath wafted a single, tired word: "home." It was barely a whisper.

Was Uncle Ray imploring him to leave? Or did he mean "home" in the sense of finding one to go to? McKellar wrestled momentarily with nuance. Was Uncle Ray asking to be taken home? Just then a pair of clawed hands clapped on his shoulders. McKellar couldn't believe the strength that forced him out of where he was sitting and onto his knees before his uncle's wheelchair. The face he looked up to was sagacious and commanding. "Get home quick," Uncle Ray said. His energy was terrible. "Pray for help, and kill the Devil on your way."

McKellar twisted out of Uncle Ray's grasp, sat back on the floor shocked. The voice went on with its own awful urgency, rattled in McKellar's head with orders to kill, to worship, to sacrifice. The old man before him shook with rage and passion, lashed out at the room with both fists over his head. McKellar felt filth and relief as the nurses arrived. Their chorus seemed both cheering and knowing. Things reassembled as if nothing had happened. McKellar still couldn't believe it. He watched the nurses wipe drool out of his Uncle Ray's beard.

Dinner at Cliff and Eva's that night was its usual mixture of forced conversation and politeness. McKellar gave up trying to cut his chicken with a knife, and lifted it to his mouth with both hands. He used only thumb and forefinger though. Felt more elegant that way. Seemed to help him keep his balance too, as the room began its first twirls. The kids giggled. He made a point of asking Eva about when Uncle Ray had started growing the hair and beard. She shot dirty glances in response, tried to move conversation elsewhere. The kids looked confused. Eva helped them cut their chicken. Cliff asked McKellar what he was going to do tomorrow. McKellar remembered seeing a magician one time pull a tablecloth off a table without disturbing any of the dishes. He felt like trying it. Instead, he adjusted his napkin, smiled pleasantly, and asked Cliff to get him another beer.

The afternoon had been a long one. Seemed like yesterday already that he had been up to the nursing home. Had come back to Eva's via the Curling Club. McKellar concentrated. "Get home quick" were Uncle Ray's exact words. Get home to what? McKellar asked himself. Home, as far as he was concerned, was Tina. Spent the afternoon telling Elwin all about it. About how he had met Tina at the Victoria Beauty Rooms in Charlottetown. She was a beauty consultant and aesthetician. Her summer job. He was supposed to pick up something for Eva. He remembered their lunches on the green at the Confederation Centre. Evenings with Tina out at Cavendish. Her long dark body. Her red toenails. "That sweetly unzipped summer of our youth"—McKellar always thought he should write a poem beginning with that line. She was first runner up in her high school beauty pageant. He followed her home to Halifax that fall. Dartmouth really, but saying Halifax made it sound as if he had a job over there. Nothing but Tina.

Cliff set a glass of beer in front of him.

McKellar wondered if he shouldn't have taken the time to marry Tina good and proper. Wondered if that would have made any difference. A pledge of love in a good suit. A good Christian house to come home to. Told Elwin that Uncle Ray had failed a good deal since he last saw him. Was still full of good advice though. He wondered if he should never have bothered with Tina at all. Elwin kept them coming.

McKellar was thinking about the strange tatoos on Uncle Ray's hands, was looking at his own palm through the beer glass when Eva interrupted: "I never expect you to listen to me, Ray," she said. "But you needn't have mentioned Uncle Ray in front of the kids."

"Where the hell are they?" asked McKellar, looking around.

"Cliff's putting them to bed; and that tone will not do in this house."

"Oh hell," McKellar returned, "meeting the old fellow would do them a world of good. They might learn something."

McKellar could still see their little faces beaming with rapt attention at the thought of having another Uncle Ray. He's the *real* Uncle Ray, McKellar told them.

Feeling a joyful diabolical freedom now, McKellar rocked himself away from the table. He stood at the foot of the stair, and hollered up in the direction of the kids' bedroom: "He's the best damned uncle in the world!" he roared. Eva put her hand on his back, and he could see Cliff starting down the stairs.

McKellar was half in tears as they sat him back down at the dining room table. He tried to explain: "You should have seen his poor old face, his poor old hands."

Eva made soothing noises.

"He spoke to me in a dream, Eva," McKellar said.

The hallway seemed to swim all around him, and McKellar was conscious of Cliff helping him into his coat. "Sure has been a long day," said McKellar offhandedly. Puffing, he leaned against the doorjamb of the front porch, was surprised at how dark it was outside. The late evening air was thick and salty. He could feel sweat on his face. "I'll drive him home," he heard Cliff's voice say from somewhere behind him.

McKellar poured himself into the tent trailer at the end of the driveway. He fumbled with the latch as he tried to get in, and the whole structure rocked dizzily. He could see lit windows across the yard; shook his fist at the house and gave a mad little kick. As a result, he fell backward onto the floor of the camper.

Home. He held the ropey musk of the canvas soft top in his nostrils, and thought about where he might find the home that Uncle Ray had endorsed. It sure as hell wasn't to be found in the house across the way. And the Devil? Neely?—whoever that was. McKellar didn't give a damn. Even Tina. McKellar had read somewhere that in seven years every cell of the body has been replaced by another cell. She was no longer the same person he had first known. It was impossible for her to be. And he wasn't the same either.

Sitting up, he noticed a pile between him and the bed. Some of his stuff had been moved out: his science fiction books, his skin magazines, some clothes, even an old ship's clock that he could never quite get to work. At the bottom was the richest prize of all: a set of musty nautical charts. The binding had all let go now, and bits of torn paper scattered as McKellar pulled the large volume across the floor toward him. On the cover it said: "World Mercator Projection: True Atlas." On the inside cover, his own name was scrawled in large childish hand. Beside it was written: "love, Uncle Ray."

He could imagine Tina carrying out his things. She never thought anything but the best of him. Perhaps he should go over and knock on the door, thank her for rounding up his stuff. The lights were still on. He laid back on the floor, relaxed, knitted fingers together to support the back of his head. Uncle Ray was so right: anger only sped up time.

Some time passed in half-awareness. McKellar thought he must have dozed off for a second. At any rate, he found himself pawing through the dusty dog-eared pages of the mercator charts. He could just barely make out detail by the light of the bedroom window facing the driveway. A dim thought in his head informed him that he was looking for a place to go, a place to call home. He traversed oceans with the flip of a page, navigated inlets with nonchalance. Now and then he'd see the tracings of indelible ink that he used to plot courses with; would see an "x" where Uncle Ray had reported being. Without helping it, he heard a childish chanting inside his head: ". . . and bless me and Mommy and Eva, and bless Uncle Ray, and make everybody good."

McKellar wondered if Uncle Ray was sleeping now. He could see again his ragged, tormented, hairy face. It was chillling. But it was reassuring too. A fellow could clean out each of the world's four corners and still get no further than the car in the yard or the trousers over the dressing chair. He thought of Tina, undressed, by the long mirror in the bedroom. He thought of Uncle Ray, aboard ship on the far side of the world and getting no closer home. McKellar felt the same way. Felt that there was a part of him that was never going home—but there was a part of him that would never leave home either. He would simply sail away in the storm of the world and put in to safe harbor when he could. Uncle Ray knew. He had tried to tell him too. And McKellar felt as if he really understood, felt that he was perfectly reconciled for the first time ever. It was a feeling he hugged to himself as he drifted away into sleep: it was before closing time at the Curling Club; it was before the bedroom lights went off in the house; it was before the dream began again.

Numbered Days

Every summer up till then had been the same: the end of classes, the trip up to the old folks' place, the long warm days, the delight of freedom from school. Now, for some reason, it was no longer the same. His days were precious, his hours, his minutes— 86,400 seconds a day were what he figured. They were not to be wasted on slow grandparents. Even Uncle Teddy seemed too old to understand. All that really mattered was getting over to the Hardy place every evening after chores were done. Marcia Hardy—that's all he knew. His longing was a discovery he held secret.

Bedtime was still early as always, his prayers said, his sleeps long. Mornings came chill and dewy. Daylight and the hum of Uncle Teddy's cream separator combined to wake him. Then he heard the opening and shutting of the screen door, the clatter of plates, radio noise. A daily chorus of activity downstairs and far away only helped lengthen out his morning slumbers. Then the squeak of the stair door, and the voice of his grandmother: "Time to get up, Ronny! Time to get up. The men are gone to the fields."

Resentment settled on his morning bones anew. His figure slumped over the breakfast table under the weight of suggestions that he sit up straight. The pain of waking had not yet left him, and he stared. Here was the everyday escapement of farm work and big meals, measured by the kitchen clocks and ticked off on the calendars. But the warmth of the stove was good and the sun had already climbed into the sky. He corrected himself; actually the earth had turned more toward the sun. It was the same every day: the hiss of bacon fat, the breakfast greeting, the weather observations, the farm commodities report on the radio. And "Ronny"—God, how he hated being called that name now. It was embarrassingly childish. He had just turned sixteen. His name was Ron.

He stood at the back gate, looked at the fields hunched together up a hill to the far woods. He could see the dew-kicked paths the cattle had made in their morning trudge toward the stable. Daily milking, he thought, what a life sentence. He followed the tractor laneway over the gully in the middle of the field. The creek there dried to a trickle every summer before he arrived. That didn't deter him from trying to catch fish in it once. He was so young, so stupid. The old folks still poked fun at him about it. A later, more adventurous summer, he tried to follow the creek bed to its source, to the consternation of a search party that found him chilled and crying under the bridge at the Trans-Canada Highway the following morning. He had given them quite a scare. Embarrassment about that episode was now tempered with a certain pride, a sense of importance grafted onto his new-found teenage sagacity. He couldn't remember a summer not spent with his grandparents and his Uncle Teddy. But their predictability had become tiresome, their concern an affront. He was experienced.

Experience was what he knew with Marcia Hardy. After breakfast was done, he would start back to the fields, cut through to the other farm and pump water. Then he would come back on the main road to pump water at the road field in front of the house. That's where they met: her jeans wrapped around one ankle, her legs in the air, their bursting flesh and, afterward, their nakedness quiet under the sun. Hidden from the road in the grassed-over foundation of what was once a house, they held each other and murmured: she, about his gentleness, his strength; he, of her smoothness and beauty. He would look at Marcia, and feel like a vaguely tragic figure—one with knowledge beyond his years. They shared a secret of insight into an exclusive adult world.

It was as if, together, they had found the meaning of life and death dictated by mutual longing. She said that girls wanted to do it just as much as guys did, but had to be more careful. He was amazed to learn that girls eyed the bulge in a guy's pants the same way that guys studied the rounded rears and budding breasts of girls. Under the guise of a summer-school project, he questioned a nurse in the hospital in Alberton about "safe" days. She didn't seem to notice the timorousness of his inquiry, responded most clinically that there were indeed safe days.

Days like today. Ron and Marcia walked hand-in-hand to the mailbox, kissed again before he started back down the lane with the newspaper. "See you tonight?" she asked, knowing full well the answer as she wiggled her fanny on the bicycle seat, mouthed a final kiss at him, and began to pedal toward home.

Marcia was a full year and two days older than he was. She had a summer job at the Stedman store in Alberton, hoped they would keep her on after the summer was over. She said she was fed up with school, and that he probably would be too after another year. Ron promised her if that were to happen, that he would move back permanently and they would get married and be in love. They would be together forever, and wear clothes only when absolutely necessary. Their bodies and the process of their discovery felt new every time. He hoped she wouldn't be late getting off work tonight.

As he walked back toward the house, Ron couldn't help thinking how precious his love for Marcia was. He thought of her as Eve, him as Adam—they were made perfectly for each other. The whole world could end so long as they remained the same. He would think of her all day as he labored under a sun of sweat and imposition. He pumped water, turned hay, drove the cattle home. He watched days on the calendar, hours on the clock. It was all a waste without Marcia to share them.

Uncle Teddy caught his eye in the mirror one night as he washed up before dinner. "Headed over to the Hardy place?" he asked.

Ron simply nodded.

After dinner, on the porch alone, his uncle pointed out that maybe he should just stay around the place for the evening. "We never spend any time together anymore," he said. "Perhaps we'll get a ball game on the radio."

Ron shook his head. "I said I was coming over this evening," he emphasized with the certainty of one who never went back on his word.

"OK," Uncle Teddy returned easily. "Just be careful."

"Careful of what?" he demanded to know.

"Just careful." Uncle Teddy gazed thoughtfully toward the road. "Don't get into any trouble."

Ron snorted a giggle as he left. Halfway up the lane he looked back and waved. Uncle Teddy seemed just like the old folks now. He couldn't understand. He couldn't know the need between he and Marcia. Ron felt a little sorry for him too. Poor Uncle Teddy, he thought, never even been married. He wondered if his uncle had ever even had girlfriends, he seemed so old. Ron put his hands in his pockets, continued down the lane, felt wise.

He wished he knew how many times he had walked up and down this lane. He knew the morning stroll with the sun on his back, the evening smell of the junipers near the road. He counted the weathered fenceposts, felt a sense of loss. He and his Uncle Teddy had always been such pals before. There was nothing Teddy could do without him wanting to be there. The old folks too, and the place itself had a hold on his younger years. He had practically been raised up here in the years before his mother got married again. He was so young then but he could still remember it now—his grandfather taking him out in a sled every morning to get the mail on this very lane, Grandma rocking him silently to sleep as she read from scripture in the evening, Uncle Teddy feeding him the milk porridge and molasses that his infant palate loved. These wellknown kindnesses were a bond. But it was a bond, he thought, that tied him to a former life of dependence and immaturity.

Being together with Marcia was a new kind of dependence, a shared dependence of daring mischief. He recalled with delight that first time they groped for each other in the darkness over the feed house. She was too shy to let him see her in the light. He was nervous too. But they swarmed with each other, and there was no turning back. Exploring further and further in the darkness, they made love, finally, in that same feed house loft. He remembered wrapping his arms around her and holding the slats of the loft floor so they wouldn't squeak. Down below, through the cracks, he could see Marcia's father filling feed dishes for the hens, counting sacks of starter meal, drinking rum out of his barn bottle. Ron could feel the sweat on his face along with the incredible leverage of their motions. It was too lovely to stop, and Marcia whispered to him that her dad was too drunk to take any notice of them anyway.

That night was a night to celebrate. They raided the old man's stash, and camp up with two pint bottles of amber rum in a bag behind one of the feed barrels. Feeling heroic, Ron tipped up one of the flasks and squeezed the hot liquid down into his throat. He wheezed with exhilaration, tears came to his eyes. He and Marcia kissed again, hard and deeply, tonguing each other's hot and sweet rum mouth. Halfway through the second bottle, he felt the earth slide under him and lost Marcia from his grasp. His stomach heaved heat up into his mouth, sudden and full; and he found that he couldn't stop himself. The agony was like death, but he could hear himself repeating into the night that he was alright. For some barely perceptible reason he didn't feel fear. Marcia went in around midnight. He made his way home blindly some time after.

Next morning found him wasted in pain at the kitchen table. Grandma said it had to be a summer flu that was going around the district. Grandpa and Teddy just ate their breakfast in silence, avoided looking at their humiliated charge. Shame and bitterness gnawed at him, but he was too miserable to care. The men left for the fields, and Ron lurched back up the stairs to bed. His grandmother took a cold cloth up to him, urged him to try and eat a little toast if he could. But he just left it on the saucer. Swore to himself that he would never drink liquor again. Snoozed. Thought: one hundred and eighty-six thousand feet per second was the speed of light, was the speed of time, was the speed that he must be going too since he was part of time. His half-sleeping mind played with the word "diurnal"—a word from last year's science class. Everything was diurnal.

He stayed in his room the rest of the morning, his stomach slumped within him like an airless bladder. He dozed lightly, gazed now and then at the outdated calendars on the walls of his room: horse and pretty girl, 1950; plaid-shirted loggers on river drive, 1959; collie with long red tongue, 1954. They seemed utterly remote from him. I wasn't even born yet in 1954, he thought to himself.

Thinking of the calendars reminded Ron of the many downstairs: the calendar from the pharmacy, from Lidstone's garage, even the one put out by the Co-op with the little thermometer on it. Grandpa watched the changing of the moons on the pharmacy calendar. Uncle Teddy wrote the day's weather on the Co-op calendar. Grandma read the daily biblical passage cited on the church calendar. How many calendars do they need? he wondered, remembering that even the wristwatch they had given him for his birthday changed dates daily.

He dug his arm out from under the sheet, watched a minute sweep by on the second hand. Gone forever, he thought. The watch felt cold on his arm. Every second was a second taken away.

He heard his name mentioned at lunch time, but he was too embarrassed to go down and show himself. After the men had cleared out, and Grandma had gone into the garden, he went down and ate at the place that had been set for him. There was no pleasure in it though. And he had never been so thirsty in his life. Still, it was long past noon and he felt recovered enough to put in some sort of appearance.

"How's the head?" Uncle Teddy asked, as he arrived in the back field.

"It's OK," he answered shortly.

The sun burned white overhead.

Teddy handed him a jar of water. "I saved you a few mouthfuls," he said.

Uncle Teddy knew. It was the same motion he had used a week or two earlier, in at the Alberton Exhibition: "Have a pull of rum, Teddy?" offered Bobby Connors. "Just a small one," he returned, and took a healthy swallow. Then, in front of Bobby Connors and the other men, he handed the bottle to his nephew. There was a collaborative smile on his face. "Don't let on to the folks now," he said.

Ron held the cool-beaded jar to his face, stood with his uncle in the shade by the edge of the wood. Together, they watched the old man turning windrows of drying hay. He worked in the middle of the field as if powered by the sun, his figure serviceable, strong, ancient. A father to one, grandfather to the other. Ron felt as though the three of them were attached by an invisible harness. And behind him, waiting to be born, was the great-grandchild, the continuance in time. Ron wondered if Grandpa would be alive to see it. He watched as his grandfather's pitchfork feathered the brittle clover, lifted it high overhead and returned it to its place on the earth. He was a part of the field and its bounty.

"The old guy's going great guns today," Teddy observed.

Ron felt his stupid thoughts betrayed, felt vain and self-conscious. He was just then wondering how long his grandfather would live.

Later, that same afternoon, he and Grandpa walked back through the line woods to the spring on Elmer Waite's property. Ron carried the empty water jar. His grandfather stopped and pointed calmly in the direction of a clearing. "There's a pretty little tree," he said. Then, as if rescuing an entangled lamb, he walked through the brush and pulled some grass and undergrowth out from around the tiny evergreen. He sized the tree and walked back to where Ron stood, and the boy was suddenly penetrated with the understanding that this year's Christmas tree had been chosen. Here, in the middle of August, he had witnessed a winter's task of preparedness, care, love. It was like a secret, and Ron wanted to put his arm around the old man, wanted to tell him how much he loved him. Only his maturity held him back.

The afternoon hummed with heat. Uncle Teddy drove the tractor while Grandpa rode on the wagon and built the load. Ron walked from stack to stack, lifted the bales and flexed, threw them in arcs through the air. He started once with a fear that stabbed him as one of the bales struck his grandfather, nearly knocked him over. But nothing was said. "Go easy now," was all his grandfather suggested, as he found a place for the bale. Ron watched him work on in his self-contained silence, sweat greasing his weathered collar, darkening the rim of his cap. Ron felt that his grandfather's strong old face knew better of his situation than he let on, and he wanted to tell him everything about his feelings for Marcia. He wanted some sort of a sign, a blessing, words of wisdom. On his birthday, Grandpa told him that being sixteen was the start of manhood. Ron asked him what age he'd be if he could have any year back he wished, and the old man answered gently that he'd be sixty again if he could. "Sixty, with all my troubles behind me," he said. Inside, Ron wished that his grandfather would never die.

It was the first summer that Ron had done meaningful work on the farm. He felt as if he now knew what "putting his back into it" meant. And he was proud of his new abilities. He carried and lifted, pitched and chucked—performed his tasks with adult resignation. He felt like a necessary part of the job to be done when he went along with Teddy to help fight fires along the Prince County Road. Anyone who could spare a day pitched in.

Marcia's brother was there too, most days. Harry was his name. He had been laid off at the Massey plant in Brantford, Ontario and had brought his whole family home for the summer. Sort of made things crowded around the Hardy place, Ron thought; and Marcia told him that the folks weren't all that pleased about him being home. Once, during a break at the fire line, Harry Hardy cocked a finger at Ron and called him a "horny little bastard," to the delight of some of the other fellows on the job. "Here now," Uncle Teddy had interjected, "that's enough of that." Ron felt relief at his uncle's intervention; impotence as well, though. Marcia's brother had walked in on them one time in her bedroom upstairs. Ron couldn't help thinking to himself what a shotgun name "Harry Hardy" was.

That evening Uncle Teddy told Ron that Harry Hardy was more to be pitied than condemned, because of his poor upbringing. He never had any schooling and old Hardy was rough on him too. Ron didn't think that Harry required any defending though, didn't look forward to meeting up with him again either. But he didn't have to face him on the job again. They took Bertha Wedge's young fellow back to the home in Charlottetown and the fires suddenly stopped.

The next time Ron saw Harry was at the Carleton Cove picnic. It was just before the set-to with Lewis McClinton. There was no telling how it got started, something of an argument about hockey. Lewis McClinton called Team Canada a bunch of assholes, said the Soviets were the best in the world and would prove it again this fall. Someone told him he was full of shit, and he pretended to think Ron had said it, pretended indignation at the gravity of the insult. In fact Ron thought the whole thing was a matter of pretense; couldn't believe what was happening, as he felt himself jostled toward the horseshoe pits. He knew Lewis was a former boyfriend of Marcia's, but didn't think that it had anything to do with him. But all he could see now was a blur of unfamiliar faces, eager with scorn. "Knock his head off, Lewis," he heard someone say, and saw Harry Hardy step in front of him with a beer in hand. "You're on your own now," he quipped.

It wasn't much of a fight. Ron was looking toward the safety of the main picnic area when the first blow was struck. He felt he was part of a bitter cartoon. Down in the pit sand, he could feel himself being kicked, covered his face. He was terrified and confused. Suddenly it all stopped. He was picked up and cleaned off by some men who had come over to break it up.

Lewis McClinton took the blame triumphantly and left with a group of his friends. Ron looked through the crowd at the victor's fat proud face, his jutting jaw, his black teeth. He looked retarded. The whole situation was without reason, and Ron wished he hadn't come, wished he had never even heard of the place. He felt wretched, humiliated, and walked away from Marcia when she tried to comfort him. "He's nothing but a big ape," she said by way of explanation as she followed him in his anguish. But Ron was tearful and disgraced. He wanted to strike out at something, wanted to destroy part of his embarrassment, especially when Marcia's brother told him that he had stood up well for a fellow who didn't have a chance.

He drove back home in the truck with his uncle, still trying to figure out what had made Lewis McClinton so ferocious. He didn't even know him. Finally, Uncle Teddy broke the brooding silence. "Some of these young fellows are always looking for trouble," he said. "They're a damned rough bunch."

So that was it. A rough bunch. He didn't matter. He was just a prop for their display of roughness. And hadn't he played the part? Allowed himself to be kicked like an empty box? He felt withered in dishonor, was sick at the notion that Teddy was a little ashamed of him. "I'd love to get another chance at him," he said. "Just he and I alone, none of his friends around."

"Be still," responded Uncle Teddy with impatience. "You did the right thing, the manly thing. Let the ignorant bastard gloat."

He thought of that whole violent episode again today as he strolled back to the fields. The gritting shame of it had eased with each internal recounting. "By their own works shall ye know them." He felt resolved. Looked at his wristwatch. Marcia would be at work by now. And still a long day ahead of him.

Today the last load of hay would be taken in. He walked the middle of the lane, satisfied in the sense of a job well done. But he was also relieved that there'd be no more chaff down the back of his neck, no more twine burns because of forgotten work gloves at the house. Soon he'd be headed home for another year of school—grade eleven. He looked forward to the specialized courses like Biology and Physics. Perhaps he'd try out for the football team.

But school still seemed far away as he felt the freshness of the open field in his chest, smelled the earthy cure of first harvest. He saw the cattle over on the other place, making their way toward the road field to drink. He watched their vacant chewing, thought their large dozy cow eyes looked curiously beautiful. Far away, he could see the tractor and wagon at the back field. His uncle and grandfather looked like stick men in the distance. He hoped that Uncle Teddy would get the binder working before he had to leave. The grain had ripened early this year in all the sunshine and he had never had a chance to help stook sheaves. He thought of Marcia again as he quickened his step, and wished the day was through.

The day rhymed away in Ron's head, accompanied by the roar of the tractor. Trips back and forth to the barn loft took on their own rhythm under a sun that seemed penetrating in its heat. It baked him. During an afternoon break, he became conscious of a long shrill monotonous drone, and Uncle Teddy commented, "It's hot when those devils start singing." Ron agreed. Thought he had read somewhere that it was actually the sound of their wings that made the noise. Cicada. Locusts. The stridulating male.

Every time he heard the word "locust" he thought of the plague of locusts in the Bible. He took a sip of water, thought about how far-removed this field was from a tormented Pharaoh of ages ago, his chin beard like a wrapped candy bar. Still the same sun though, thought Ron looking up. The same sun that the Pharaohs saw, that everyone who had ever lived had seen.

He flexed and lifted all afternoon, bared his back to the overhead sun against the advice of his uncle and grandfather. He wrapped his shirt like a turban around his head, sat cross-legged on the top of the loaded haywagon. It had been piled extra high and Ron rode it as if he were a conqueror. It was the last load to be taken in that summer.

He could see all the back fields from the top of the wagon: the Waite place, Roger Gallant's, even the Hardy place. He savored the thought of holding Marcia to him again. With cavalier abandon, he looked up directly into the sun, challenged it with Marcia on his mind. He felt strong, a match for the sun that burned itself into him. He had heard that a person would go blind if he looked directly at the sun every day for a week. Ron wondered if anyone had ever actually done it for proof. He looked back down at the moving ground under him, saw fluttering silver spots and a purple hole in his vision where the sun had made its imprint.

He thought how terrible it would be to be blind, to never see Marcia's beautiful face again. But then he thought that now that he had seen it, he could never forget. He could still see her fresh face and rose-pillowed lips pouting in a silent kiss. Ron hoped that someday they could be together all the time, be naked together under this same sun here in the back fields. He wanted this load of hay off and into the barn, himself washed, fed, and over at the Hardy place.

But a surprise waited for them in the yard: a big black sedan with two tall, well-dressed men. They were clean-shaven and smiling, and announced greeting with smiles that made one immediately wary. They had the assertive confidence of relatives from the States, but Ron noticed Teddy bypassing all greetings as he disappeared into the house after getting the tractor stopped. "Mr. W. H. MacLeod?" one of them said, extending his hand to Ron's grandfather. He sounded relieved to have finally met him, as if he had been searching especially for him.

"My name's Derek Armitage," the man went on, "and this is my partner in Christ, Gary King." Ron knew they had to be religious types, it was something in their bearing, in their well-washed authority. They were members of the New Testament Crusaders, they said; announced that their worldwide mission was to stop all wars and relieve mankind from famine. Some of their top people had already met with world leaders. Their voices were raised and cheerful, seemingly unperturbed by the dire topics with which they dealt.

They were conversational about the glories of good weather, the bounty of nature, the blessings of a beautiful place like "P. E. Island," as they called it. They were even interested in the condition of the crops around Prince County, but were quick to point out that the rest of the world cringed in starvation and terror by contrast. One of them noted that there were child prostitutes in big cities that were "no older than this boy here," as he placed a hand on Ron's shoulder.

Grandpa agreed that the world was in a terrible state, then looked significantly at his grandson who took a step away quickly from under the man's grasp.

Uncle Teddy returned with a dipper of water but the two Crusaders declined his offered drink. "We're nourished by the Lord," one of them said.

Ron drank gladly after his grandfather. He felt the dried shingles of his throat ease with the water, thought that this tiny barnyard was rather far removed from the hokey geography lesson that these missionaries had to teach. He was offended by their perfect elocution and unabashed vitality—they sounded like they were teaching grade one Sunday school. Most of all, though, he was embarrassed by the cowed aspects of his uncle and grandfather, by their silent audience as these dapper salesmen continued their list of the world's atrocities. When one stopped, the other started—it was like a monologue for two. They even seemed to be wearing the same suit.

Finally they asked for help to carry on their mission, and Ron's grandfather reached into his pocket almost automatically. The men accepted a few wrinkled bills. "Is it enough?" Grandpa asked.

"Every bit helps," was the response.

"Join me in prayer," one said.

All heads bowed automatically.

But Ron held his head up, looked at the dark, surrendered forms of his uncle and grandfather. He felt the same anguish and indignation he had felt at the Carleton Cove picnic.

As the prayer ended, one of the men looked up to the sky and asked for special strength. Then they shook hands all around, their grips firm and triumphant. Ron tried purposely not to meet their eyes. "Our days are numbered on the earth," one of them said. "He who knows the very numbers of hairs on our heads, knows also the number of days appointed for each of us to walk this earth."

Ron felt that he had known this all along. He felt that the New Testament Crusaders were only stating the obvious. They have the gall to say what others keep decently to themselves, he thought as he caught again their unfading smiles, their colored neckties. He felt like shouting swear words at them as they got into their big car. The plates were white and black with the word "SAVED" on them instead of numbers. Ron wondered what province they were from.

"There's a couple of those preachers come through every year," said Uncle Teddy as he and Ron began handling the final load of bales.

Ron fumed in silence, looked at his watch, thought of the time that had been lost. There was a whole wagon to unload, dinner to eat, and chores to get done before he could get over to Marcia's place. He felt robbed.

"They can be a nuisance sometimes with all their Bible talk," Teddy continued. "Still, it never hurts to be friendly."

It was almost dark by the time he made it over to the Hardy place that evening. The house and buildings looked unreal from the road, cast in the last throes of daylight. Behind them and over the water, clouds billowed up purple and threatening. Ron noticed for the first time the broken weather vane on the barn roof, thought that a good rainfall might cool things down a bit.

Harry and Mr. Hardy watched him walk in from the road. They sat on an old car seat on the front porch drinking beer. A couple of Harry's dirty-faced little kids wrestled in the dust of the yard. They ran to the safety of the porch as he drew near. One of the many dogs around the place got up, shook itself, and growled at his approach.

He was told that Marcia wasn't home, that she had gone off to the drive-in in Alberton with some of her friends.

Ron stood there in silence for a few moments. He watched a couple cars go by. She left right after dinner, they said. Didn't know what time she'd be back.

Refusing the offer of a beer, Ron started away from them. He felt his face go awkward, could feel the grinning faces behind him burning into his back. He walked out to the road the way he had come, the dog barking his retreat. He looked back at the place with contempt, at the old engine blocks and rusting auto frames that sat in the yard by the barn. Marcia wouldn't have been home no matter what time he had arrived. He felt a terrible sense of waste, of shame and betrayal.

A couple days later, Marcia told him about the guy she had been going with in Alberton, and about how she'd had to choose him since Ron would be going back to school in Charlottetown that fall. "His name is Ron too," she said, adding that because of what they had shared she could never love anybody whose name was not Ron. Like her, he worked in the Stedman store and was hoping to be put on manager trainee course.

Ron didn't know what to reply. He didn't think choice entered into the matter. It was love. But Marcia seemed so matter-of-fact about it all now that she even looked different to him. Ron could hardly believe that he had ever seen her naked.

Later that same night, he slumped in the easy chair in the sitting room of his grandparents' house. He thought about Marcia and about how many excuses he had made to himself about her ordinariness. Her silences no longer seemed alluring to him but a mark of drab uncon-cern, a mark of the stunning dumbness he had met everywhere that summer.

He felt dumb too. Only the mantle clock across the room had something to say. The only truths there were, were to be heard in its incessant repetitions. Ron looked at the Roman numerals on the clock face, felt like a romantic martyr to the spirit of loss as he wondered what girls would be in his class that fall.

But it was his immediate surroundings that attracted his attention most fully. He watched as Uncle Teddy recorded the day's weather on the Co-op calendar. Grandpa rocked in the chair by the radio, read the newspaper. Grandma sat by the light on the table, looked through a couple of pamphlets left by the New Testament Crusaders. Ron was struck again by what he felt he had always known, that all their days upon the earth were numbered: Grandpa's, his, Marcia's, everybody upon the earth living at that very moment, everybody who had ever lived. He felt he had plenty more days to go, though, and kissed his grandmother on his way up to bed.

The Governor of
Prince Edward Island

Walter Patterson had run the lobster suppers at
the church hall in New Dublin for years. On account of his name—the
same name as the Island's first colonial governor—the nightly affair
had come to be known as "The Governor's Feast." A radio station in
Charlottetown first coined the name; tourists seemed to like it. The
name was doubly appropriate too, because "Governor" or "Gov" was
what Patterson had been called most of his life anyway. If you called
him "Walter," he'd probably wonder who you were talking to.

Way back when, it was Gov Patterson who had applied for the
hall's restaurant license. Again, when the hall expanded, it was the
Governor who oversaw the project, from the application for government support to the last strip of metal siding. No job was too small for
his personal attention. Over the years, he had come to love the detail:
the number of persons at a sitting, the variety of places represented by
tourists on any given evening, the accounts receivable, even the weight

of lobsters consumed. He never left without being the one to turn out the lights at night; was always first one over on Sunday mornings to arrange things for tea time after early service. Throughout winter, the Governor called bingo numbers on Thursday nights. He seemed to be always in charge without exerting control.

Under Gov Patterson's guidance, the lobster suppers had become New Dublin's claim to fame. For six nights every week in the summer tourists enjoyed flocking to the church hall, blenching at the red claws and antennae on their plates, and being a part of traditional Maritime hospitality. Ever moving from kitchen to tables, the Governor's compact and well-dressed form seemed overseer of the event. He was everywhere. The only summer his energy flagged was the one when the Department of Tourism provided old-time musicians and a fat actor in colonial garb to heighten revelry at the feast. This dramatic flair only detracted from the basic homeliness of the suppers though, and a petition from the New Dublin Ladies' Aid asked that the entertainment be discontinued. Gov Patterson wrote the cover letter, said that they wanted the lobster suppers—feastlike or not—to remain small and unencumbered, with a certain local dignity. The next thing you know, they'll be trying to license the hall for serving liquor, he pointed out to a meeting of the lobster supper trustees. Everyone in New Dublin signed the letter, whether or not they shared Gov Patterson's personal disdain.

As has been so often pointed out, over pulls of rum in barn lofts and oyster shacks, the public consumption of alcohol is not all that contrary to the Island way of life. In fact the first Legislative Assembly of Prince Edward Island convened in a tavern in 1770, and was presided over by Governor Walter Patterson, Colonel-retired of His Majesty's 80th Foot. Then, from his office in a different Charlottetown tavern, Governor Patterson began the long and fraudulent process of dispersing absentee-held property. But the present-day "Governor" Patterson would have no part of the deceit and raucousness that liquor inevitably invited. He abstained, and felt sorry for anyone who didn't, as his mother had taught him when she was still living. She died of pneumonia one winter after Walter's father, in a drunken rage, had locked her out of the house. From her deathbed, she had taught the boy never to backtalk, always to be civil, and never to touch liquor. Even though his father had "the sickness," as she called it, Walter would be spared it if he always remembered that a soft answer turneth away wrath. At the graveside after his mother's funeral, Gov Patterson took the pledge from

Mr. Johnstone, the Baptist minister. His Aunt Agnes and Aunt Bethany each held one of his hands. He was twelve years old.

Gov Patterson's only slip in over fifty years occurred about a month later. His father hadn't drawn a sober breath since a week before the funeral, and the boy found himself attracted in curiosity to the dirty brown liquid his father was constantly swilling down. The offer of a drink to his mother's memory was so offhand, seemed so friendly and masculine that the boy accepted, grateful for the attention. "We're still waking that good woman's memory," his father crowed, as Walter gagged on his first sip. But the old man just laughed, clapped him on the back, and took him under his tutelage with suggestions for gritting his guts and putting himself in the proper frame of mind. Some of his father's cronies arrived and cheered him on to drink after drink. He felt his chest protrude, his shoulders square; thought he had accomplished some part of manhood, or something—then the liquor hit him like a fist.

The next thing he knew, he was being lifted out of a neighbor's horse stable by Mr. Johnstone. He remembered being carried up the front steps of the manse too, and of thinking to himself at the time that the minister's house really was God's house. Then he slipped into blackness again. He was sick for nearly two days after, and luxuriated in the pillow bed and airy room to which he was confined. Everything was colored pink and decorated with flowers, and the ceiling of the room was so high up he knew he'd need a ladder to reach it. Mrs. Johnstone read to him from the children's Bible stories, served him broth, called him an angel. She seemed more like an older sister than a mother, and the Governor thought that she was the most beautiful woman alive; thought too, that she was about half the age of Mr. Johnstone. They played "I spy" and charades, and the minister talked about putting the boy in a foster home. But the Gov cried and begged to be sent home to his own father rather than somewhere strange. He swore that he would never be sick again, that he would work for God to cure his father. Mrs. Johnstone and he both cried when he left, and the minister shook his hand as if he were an associate. The Governor promised to be a good boy, all the while recounting his injuries inside and promising himself that he would grow up to make his father pay. It was a boy's ferocity that the Governor fairly laughed at in recalling these days.

He could recount and embellish his childhood abuse with great irony, and it made him much sought after as host and speaker. There's nothing the Governor liked better than a bit of spiced drollery. To business or political meetings, he enjoyed recalling how his father used to cut chewing tobacco into his food so he could get accustomed to the taste. It got so bad that the Governor was throwing up more than he was taking in, and Dr. Phillips called his father an idiot to his face. As a postscript, the Governor would add that his father was a great cook— had to be, he claimed, to get him to eat that stuff in the first place. At weddings, he would compare himself to his historical namesake—no relation, of course—and joke about the original Governor of the colony along with his string of paramours from Quebec City to Washington. The man was ahead of his time in diplomacy, Gov Patterson would declare to the families of the bride and groom, never letting on how he missed his own sweetheart, Laverne Bulmer, who had married an Air Force pilot and had flown away somewhere. To the actors at the Summer Festival in Charlottetown, who considered a lobster supper following dress rehearsal to be a singular mark of good luck, Gov Patterson liked to point out that he considered himself a bit of an actor, that he could bring on tears at will. No one could outdo him in childhood anguish, he claimed. He recalled how, as a boy, he would dive under the blankets of his bed and cry out with real tears as his father beat him. The belt would come down with a resounding slap, and the Governor claimed he used to wail with such conviction that his father would ask in fear if he should get the doctor. He would have the old man at his beck and call for about a week over it even though, with the blanket padding, he never felt a thing.

The Governor would pause between stories and sip on a tall glass of ice water—his "Governor's Gin," as he liked to call it, although everyone knew he never touched a drop. Often in these silent intervals, the sweat of exertion in the smile of his face, he would recall the *real* anguish of the situation: how his father slapped him so hard once that he heard his neck crack and he was unable to focus his eyes for reading until the following day. Often, out of a perceived terror or just before a beating, his father's fury would frighten him so that he would feel a cold hole in his stomach and piss in his pants. The Governor was sent to his room one time and starved there for two days in constant anticipation of a beating. When he finally emerged, his father told him he could have come out any time he wished. It was about this time that his mother had been locked out of the house. The Governor could recall any of his childhood's hateful episodes at will: the curses in the dark of his parents' bedroom next to his, the beatings and shrieks, his mother's pleadings. He would cry real tears then, and in his mind pretend that Laverne Bulmer was erasing the blackboard at school. When she was done, the fighting would always be over. Then followed the gentle words and murmurs of repair that only seemed to hurt him more. He would lay awake in sweat, his head pounding with the fatigue of tears and confusion.

He would recall the feeling anytime; as he did at his father's funeral. The old man had finally taken one horn too many: "a fine condition in which to meet your Maker," observed the Governor wryly. People thought his humor was just a mask for his sorrow, but to the Governor it was all a matter of relief. Still, he prayed deeply for the sake of the old man's soul, prayed that they would meet again in a perfection of love and understanding impossible to be had on earth. He laid his father to rest alongside the grave of his mother, joked with the new minister about Mr. Johnstone's grave being nearby: "Father can use all the help he can get," he said. The Gov still returned to the cemetary once or twice a year just to remember.

After he was left on his own, he turned all his energy to the lobster suppers, and that's when the feast really began to grow. So did the Governor's responsibilities: it was through this time that he worked his way up from toilet scrubber to high-class restaurateur. But no one could begrudge him his success. The church hall at New Dublin was the first unlicensed establishment to be mentioned in *Where to Eat in Canada*. Gov Patterson had been named "Islander of the Year" a few years later, and was Grand Marshall of the Lobster Carnival parade in Summerside the year after that. *Weekend Canada* had even done a piece on him called "The 'Governor' of Prince Edward Island and his Lobster Supper Domain." He was surprised that half of the article appeared to be poking fun at the place; and the photograph of him holding up an impaled lobster at each side of his face looked a little cruel, he thought. The photographer had tried to get him to wear a wig such as a colonial governor might have worn, but the Gov made it clear that he wanted no part of that. He finally agreed to wear a big white chef's hat for the picture, even though he thought it looked a little silly. But it entertained everyone for miles around, and he heard that the cafeteria in the Provincial Legislature had a framed copy of that picture on the wall. The Gov was pleased when people were happy and appreciated their meal. He liked to think of himself as a benevolent servant at life's feast.

The trouble would've never happened if Governor Patterson had been listened to in the first place. He worked hard to get the nightly suppers built up to a point where they were actually breaking even in the ledger, but the Department of Tourism recommended that they be expanded. Things never stay small enough for effective management. The project called for six double-bed units to be added on to the hall. A local initiatives project was set up with matching federal and provincial funds, and the Governor found himself in the hotel business. He had been the only member of the New Dublin Lobster Suppers Association who voted against the idea.

Once the work got underway, it was hard to argue against it. The government fellows called it "ongoing," and it did provide needed winter employment. The beauty of the project was that it would provide jobs in the future too: upkeep, domestic services, further restaurant needs. The government paid for it all, so Gov Patterson just applied himself to seeing that all went smoothly. Still, he couldn't help thinking that it was all a little out of control: the hammering, the shouting, the seeming lack of organization. Half the time it stormed too hard for work to be done; other times, fellows would show up drunk and sit around most of the day doing nothing.

But the addition to the church hall was finally completed, and even the Governor had to admit that they'd done a good job. He was on hand when Miss P.E.I., Karen McKinley—later to be Miss Canada—cut the ribbon to officially open the place. The Premier made a big speech, declaring the place to be a model of hospitality as the Island's tourist industry forged ahead toward the twenty-first century. From the podium, he even held one of the Governor's hands up in the air as if he were a champion boxer, called him the man most responsible for the success of the project. Miss P.E.I. gave him a kiss on the cheek. Earlier that day the Governor had put a Bible in each of the guest rooms; prayed silently for the success of the venture.

The biggest change that the expanded hall presented to the Governor was the fact that he could no longer be the last one to lock up the place at night. He had to entrust it to a night desk, to some youngster on a summer job. It was also strange to him to see so many different faces around the place, almost as if he had lost the hall forever. But the Governor soon adjusted. He genuinely liked people, always had a friendly greeting for any of the guests, always took a final midnight walk down the hallway of the guest area before going home to bed himself. Every morning, he would arrive back to help see that the guests got a full P.E.I. breakfast.

It was on one of these late-night walk throughs that the Governor heard a curious noise. Sounded like a woman's voice. He ceased his tread on the carpeted floor, listened in half-sickened anticipation. He could just make out the low tones of a male voice in anger; then a woman's high-pitched response. They sounded like hate. Then, a shriek. Gov Patterson felt blood jump into his face, hurried down to the night desk to check the register for room 4. Mike & Minnie White, Erie PA., was what he read there. Such a distance to travel and then ruin with arguments, thought the Governor to himself as he trod the stairs again. Perhaps it was just a passing remark, a quick release of tension. Or maybe they were being sarcastic with each other, saying mean things that they really meant as tender—the way people will. But he could hear them again before even getting to the top of the stair. What must the other guests think? It sounded like he was killing her in there. There was a crash, a shriek, and another sound of something hitting the wall. The Governor knocked on the door. There was silence. He thought he could hear crying. Then another shriek, and the Governor could see his hand shaking as he inserted his pass key into the door. He saw the woman's face: fear, blood, her hair tangled, her slip. The man sat with his back to the door, his body large, angry. He swung around; and the Governor grabbed a long-necked bottle off the counter, felt the room move past him as he resolved to silence the anger, quell the pain. He could hear screams louder and louder, as he struck out again and again.

J.P. Forbes Q.C. had handled all the business for the church hall, ever since it had received its restaurant license. His office on Kent St. looked out over the park in front of the Victoria Hotel. "Who's to say what goes on behind closed doors," he said. The Governor just sat there, looked at the book-covered walls of the office. "Mrs. White's lawyer advises me that the injuries have kept her husband off work all winter," Forbes continued. "She'll testify that your action was unprovoked."

The Governor had met with Forbes months before, just after the incident occurred. He still didn't know what to say. "I don't know what made me do it," he repeated.

Forbes waved a match over his pipe. He countered that anyone with the same upbringing and violent life experiences as the Governor would probably react the same way in similar circumstances. "It's all a matter of prior cause," he said with assurance. "Innocence or guilt really isn't the issue here. The question is what anyone else would do at the time under the same circumstances."

"What about the Whites?"

"They've got insurance."

The Governor was silent, felt shamed.

"Look," Forbes went on, "we're going to plead guilty, we're going to face the judge alone without a jury, and we're going to get a suspended sentence owing to the circumstances of the event."

Forbes had been working on the case for months. In fact, it seemed almost a lifetime ago that all the trouble had occurred. The Governor had been released on his own recognizance and had been told to stay away from the church hall. He found the time awfully long, wanted to get it all over with. Sitting there in Forbes' office, the Governor found it hard to believe that he had actually done the thing that he knew himself to be guilty of. Inside, he wanted to return to the suppers, to pretend none of this had ever happened. But he knew nothing would ever be the same again.

What shocked him most when he finally came to trial was that he didn't even recognize the Whites. They could have been anybody in the world; certainly anybody other than his victims. They were even relatively friendly, and the Governor saw Forbes laughing together with their lawyer. It was almost as if he wasn't in court at all. But a fellow before him had been fined for running his car on marked gas, and Forbes had to represent another young fellow who had gotten into a fight at the Morell Legion. Deep down, the Governor felt a little victimized himself. Everything had an air of illusion about it.

The Governor wasn't really all that sure about the reality of his own trial either. On behalf of the Whites, their lawyer presented hospital receipts, physician's reports, insurance claims. Everything seemed to be contained in papers and "briefs." But, even though no arguing seemed to be involved, nothing about the morning was "brief" at all. Forbes spent a good deal of time verifying dates on various documents. In the interests of his client, he pointed out that he would refuse to proceed without being precise. The delays were exasperating. It seemed as though date, time, and place, were more important than what violence the Governor had actually perpetrated. But Forbes presented written submissions too: a letter from the cabinet secretary to the Minister of Tourism, confirming that Walter Patterson of New Dublin, P.E.I. did indeed fit the job description of "cultural diplomat;" there was a letter from the Kobe School for Girls, Osaka, Japan that attested to the nature of the Governor's reputation, as did a letter from the head office of the Boy Scouts of Canada, recounting Gov Patterson's service as Akela for the local Wolf Cub pack.

The Governor daydreamed about the little Japanese girls whom he had conducted around Cavendish and Avonlea. They were all prize-winning essayists on *Anne of Green Gables*. Seemed to be an important part of their schooling over there. They were pretty and curious little things. All of them wore glasses. The Kobe school had even invited him to Osaka for a visit. He dreamed also of his days with the cubs, the long hikes, the religious instruction. Some had grown up to be quite the successes; all credited the Governor for his patience and guidance. He loved teaching and talking, watching them grow up. Young Dr. Phillips had finally made him cut back on his responsibilities, but the Wolf Cub pack still had him as guest of honor every year at the Father and Son banquet, held usually at the church hall in New Dublin.

The whole time he was thinking back over past pleasantries, Forbes had been quietly impugning Mrs. White's character. Another letter from the Bureau of Vital Statistics, Harrisburg, Pennsylvania, indicated that she had been divorced twice before on the grounds of physical abuse. The Governor noted for the first time that Forbes used the word "indicated" an awful lot. "Didn't this indicate" Forbes asked in the coolest tone possible "that Mrs. White had both a history of and penchant for violence?" The Governor could hardly believe his ears when Forbes began to paint her as the real villain of the piece, began to describe her satisfaction as her husband received his due. The Governor looked down at the floor, studied the unremitting pattern of the carpet, tried to imagine Laverne Bulmer erasing the blackboard at school. His face in his hand felt as if it were burying into a pillow and, high up in his sinuses, he could smell tears.

Weeks intervened between final submissions and actual sentencing. On the day Gov Patterson finally heard the judge's verdict, he was accompanied by an articling clerk from Forbes' office. The White's couldn't get back to P.E.I. for the finale. Sort of made the Governor wonder why he couldn't have been informed by mail as well. The entire process had never seemed much more than a detached committee meeting to him. He wasn't even sure if this was the same judge as the last time. Anyway, he was given the suspended sentence that Forbes had predicted; ordered to pay Mrs. White a lump sum restitution of $2,500 Canadian toward her husband's medical bills. Court costs were "forgiven," and the same defense fund that paid Forbes took care of the Governor's fine. The Governor never fully understood where the money in his defense fund had come from. He figured the trustees at the church hall must have helped. But through the delays, the submissions and counter submissions, a year had nearly passed, and the Governor no longer saw anything as other than relative to something else.

The only thing certain to come out of the proceedings, was that the Governor was over 65 and receiving the old age pension. Part of Judge Doiron's decision included the recommendation that the Governor be "relieved" of any responsible connection with the New Dublin Lobster Suppers Association. This was felt by the Governor to be the *real* verdict. His actual guilt had been delayed and examined out of existence. Time and talk heals all wounds. The whole exercise was an attempt to smooth over matters and make them livable. What he had done was a matter of society; who he was made the only difference, was the only basis for argument. And the Governor never felt this split feeling as strongly as when Cyril McNair, editor of the *Prince County Journal,* ran two editorials the day after sentencing: one decried the loss of the tourist industry on P.E.I. if unprovoked attacks continued on American visitors; the other amounted to a biography and character testimony on behalf of Governor Patterson.

People continued to greet him on the street. Many let him know what they thought of the "dirty turn" that had been done toward him. But he never seemed to attract any real allegiance. It was as if he had no more stories to tell. He watched T.V., read the paper, sat at home. He complained to the few people that did drop by that he felt as if he were in a jail without bars. Now and then he would dress up the way he used to when he ran the lobster suppers or called bingo numbers. It made him feel important, he said. Sometimes he felt as if he should just go over to the hall, pay his money, and enjoy a feed like anyone else. But he knew he could never do it. He could never go back. He knew the place too well. It was as if the farm had been sold out from under him, he said. Said too that the original Governor Patterson had lost all his property in much the same way years ago. It was a new story he would tell to the next banquet he was invited to speak at.

But no more invitations came to the Governor. He seemed to slip away quietly. The only visits he made were to the manor in Summerside to visit old Mrs. Johnstone. He felt as though she was the closest person to him now, even though she was often a little confused as to exactly who he was. But it didn't matter. When certain, she usually thought of him as a twelve-year-old "angel." And the Governor would say nothing to dissuade her; would just hold one of her bunched little hands in his, and read to her from the Book of Psalms.

He felt like a living exile, he said. The way the original Governor Patterson must have felt, recalled to England in disgrace so many years ago. He felt it in the mornings as he knotted his tie in front of the mirror; in the evenings as he ate alone. He too was a banished Governor, old in his deceit of years but inside still praying for goodness sake like a little boy. His proudest boast had always been that he had never hurt anybody, but he knew it was no longer true. His atonement lay in the dead pools of contemplation that each long day afforded, in every voice that greeted him as "Governor," in every face that just as quickly took its leave.

The Promised Land

The power hadn't been out five minutes before the phone rang. I would've just as soon let it go, but Shirley got up and answered it. The tone of her voice out in the hall told me that Chester Gordon was on the line. Who else? No doubt he'd have something for me to do even on a night like this.

I pressed my face into the warm depression left by Shirley's body, wondered what Chester's topic would be for this evening: the uncivilized nature of P.E.I. snowstorms? the inconvenience of power outages? the incompetence of the Department of Highways? Wilmot Shore had been snowed in three times already this winter—once for nearly a week—and we hadn't even reached Christmas yet. "How in hell am I going to move potatoes if I can't even get out to the rail station?" Chester demanded one time of Lloyd Archibald, Minister of Highways. "I've got men to pay and potatoes to ship, but I can't do either if this road isn't cleared." I watched him hum a few grudging agreements into the telephone. Then he slammed the receiver down. "By Jesus," he said, looking in my direction, "if we'd have returned a government member, they'd be plowing this road out as if it were gold."

Whatever Chester's problem was this time, he didn't have Shirley on the line for very long. I was just picturing him again trying to get the unlisted number for the government garage in Charlottetown, when Shirley hopped back into bed beside me. There was nothing to do during these stormy evenings but nestle into bed early and let nature do the warming. Her slim body shuddered and I surrounded her with mine; felt us sharing the weight of the blankets. I didn't want to know about Chester Gordon, didn't want to know about anything, just wanted Shirley to know how much I wanted her.

But Shirley didn't seem all that interested now. She simply stated that Chester was out of kerosene and her clipped manner left me in the dark to ponder the consequences. I knew the time wasn't right, looked across the bed at the luminous dial of the clock. What the hell, I thought to myself, it isn't even bedtime anyway. I figured I might as well help the old fellow out; knew there were a pair of kerosene lamps somewhere out in the old house.

Shirley drew the blankets up tightly around her as I sat up at the edge of the bed. The fire had gone out in the kitchen and it felt cold enough to freeze tea. I told this to Shirley but she made no response beyond tucking her knees up closer under the quilts. Her back was to me and I ran a hand over her tiny form. I fixed an image of her sleeping face in my mind. Still, there was a pinch of rejection in my chest just then as I reached down for my boots. Rejection and concern too. The only thing worse was the chill of the room. Even the glow of the candle on the bedstead seemed cold. It wasn't that I minded working for Chester Gordon—he paid a living wage—and I certainly appreciated the lot at the road that he had given Shirley and me, but an interruption like this in the middle of action? It was almost inhuman. Struck me as kind of funny though, as long as I didn't think about what Shirley had said: "Perhaps you could drop a match in the homestead by accident some night."

The old guy has got no one to turn to now but me, I thought to myself. I'm the only relation left to him in the world and we're not even blood relatives at that. He and his brother were orphaned young and brought up by my grandparents. After years out west, where he struck it rich, Chester had finally landed back in the old Gordon homestead. Took full possession of the place after Wilfred passed away. Father worked for him for years, and after he died I became Chester's right-hand man—so to speak: Chester was minus one leg, and too weak to stand on the other now. Couldn't get around too well in the winter conditions. I lifted him into bed every night, wheeled him out to breakfast every morning. Wished right now that I was back in bed with Shirley.

But Chester relied on me. Relied on me at this end of the country at least. He still owned property out in B.C. Had a man named Bill who managed his farm out there, just as I did back here. I had even said hello to him one time on the phone. Chester told me that I should go out west and meet Bill some day. He said I should look the Cowichan Valley over and tell him what I thought of the place. "You'll own property out there soon enough," he'd say to me when feeling sorry for himself. "Best you should go out there and decide what to do with it." I'd always change the subject to more immediate matters, even though I loved to hear Chester describe the place out there. He said that it was on the coast rainforest of Vancouver Island, which made it sound kind of exotic and jungle-like to me. It was lush and green, had a great growing season, plenty of sun and rain, and the snow knew well enough to stay up in the mountains where it belonged. "That's the problem with P.E.I.," he said to me once. "There's no mountains. If there were, perhaps we could train the snow to go there."

Of course there were always fellows who would argue with him that snow was "the poor man's fertilizer," or that a good snowbank made best insulation against the winter's cold. But Chester wouldn't hear of it, declared B.C. to be a veritable "promised land" compared to the long winters and late springs on P.E.I. Besides, he said that by owning property at each end of the country he felt he was doing his part for national unity. He had married a woman out there years ago but, so far as I knew, never had any kids. Sort of made me his heir. He often mentioned how thankful he was that there was no "fruit of his former union." Said that his biggest mistake in a life of errors was marrying a woman so much younger than he was. "I don't know where she is now," Chester once said to a group of men over at the garage. "She's probably in Vancouver or somewhere in the States—but wherever it is you can be sure that she's driving down the price of screwing."

I chuckled to myself again just thinking about it, as I fished a flashlight out of the kitchen counter. Had to fight every inch of the way across the lane to the old house. The snow was knee-deep already, and the wind cut like a roaring rasp. I found it easier to see where I was going with the flashlight off; squinted my eyes against the storm; looked down the lane toward the Gordon homestead. It looked desolate, and I felt a little sorry for Chester alone upstairs in the dark. Sort of renewed my quest as I kicked the frost out of the old house door, tried to think where those two kerosene lamps could be.

But it was easy to get sidetracked in the old house—even on a night such as this. My grandparents had built the place and lived in it nearly a century ago. A one-room shack with an earthen floor. Neither I nor my father had ever used it for anything but storage. And yet Father had been born in the place. Perhaps until his dying day he still visualized it as a "house." Together, we had hauled the place over to Chester Gordon's years before. I kicked wood chips against the large block in the middle of the floor, eyed the pile of kindling and the stacked firewood. A workbench ran along the length of one wall now, covered in cans of nuts and bolts, old wire, scattered tools. There were spare parts for farm machinery and old cars, layers of rotten burlap, axe handles hung to dry, and shovels that stood together rusting in the far corner. I surveyed it all in the blue light of darkness as my eyes adjusted. Listened to the wind whistle in the eaves of the old house. For some reason, I felt right at home just then—like every other broken tool or discarded engine part in the place.

My discontentment always seemed to build up over time. Why in hell couldn't Chester wait out the darkness like everybody else? It was no emergency; he had his phone to talk to. No doubt he'd have had the electric company on the line by now, perhaps even spoken to the Maritimes Weather Office in Halifax. But Shirley's words came back to me again—"Light a fire by accident"—and I shook my head with bitterness. There was no point being hypocritical about it. I had thought of having the place all to myself plenty of times. And Shirley was not a cruel person. Like anyone, she said things that she didn't really mean. I often thought that life would be easier for us if I didn't have to jump every time Chester called. But whenever I caught myself thinking this way, I settled down quickly by remembering that I wasn't up to the level of administration that Chester was. I had never done much travelling; anyone I knew lived along the shore road and I certainly wasn't up to ordering the Minister of Highways to dig out the road in front of my house as if the man had a shovel in his office and was waiting to do the job. If Chester was gone, I wouldn't know where to begin. He kept a grading crew on all winter and I ran the warehouse like something of a foreman. But, like my father, I was better at taking orders than giving them. I had always worked, even if it was only to get this for Chester, get that for Chester. He was used to giving orders, and right now it was light that he was in need of. I'd get that for him too.

Father's loyalty must have rubbed off on me, I thought, as I gazed out the window of the old house. The sky had cleared although clouds still scudded along the horizon over the strait. Pinpricks of light glimmered in whisps of drifting snow. Stars on a night like this would always bring to Father's mind early-morning sled rides to the mud digger at West Creek when he and Chester were boys. They would ride together in the mud box, half awake and warmed by the jug of coffee lying between them. He said that Chester and he used to look up in the crackling pre-dawn sky and name the stars after people they knew. Sometimes, when it wasn't too cold, they'd skate on the frozen creek while Grandpa waited his turn at the scoop. The bells of the horse harness would jingle and he and Chester would take turns at the reins all the way home. All the way home with a load of steaming silt from off the river bottom to nourish the land. Must have looked ugly spread over the snow, I thought. But it was good for the fields, good for seasons to come. It was the long view of matters that was important. I looked out past the lane.

Across the way, I could see that there was a light in our kitchen window. Shirley's face appeared in the glow of the candle and she looked right at me in the dark window of the old house that she knew to be directly opposite. I was thankful that my flashlight was out, that she couldn't see me. In fact, she could see nothing but the night. I, on the other hand, could see nothing but her. She looked a little perplexed. Probably wondered what I was up to. Then she yawned— beautifully, obliviously. Like an angel, I thought; like an angel chorister on a greeting card singing the cry of "hosanna."

Just then I was interrupted by lights on the lane. A truck turned in and plowed its way through the snow, its windshield wipers flapping uselessly against the weather. It was Myles, Shirley's brother. I motioned him in with the flashlight as if I were on an airplane runway.

"Jesus, what a night!" he whooped, as he stepped inside the door of the old house.

"Not at all fit," I agreed.

"Oh yes, but I find it all very invigorating." His face beamed, and he clapped himself on the shoulders, stamped the snow off his feet.

For a second I felt a little embarrassed about being alone out in the dark of the old house. I felt as if my precious reverie had been exposed somehow, wondered what Myles must have thought I was doing. "I'm trying to search out a pair of kerosene lamps," I said; sounded guilty and added, "I know there's a couple out here somewhere."

"Plenty of time for that," Myles answered. "Have a horn?"

I accepted the bottle, felt my teeth nearly freeze to my lips and then let go as the rum slipped past into my throat. Must have been colder than I thought, because the warmth of the liquor began to crawl up my spine and my nose became runny. I took a second swig.

"Why in hell would you be searching out those old relics on a night like this?" Myles asked.

"For Chester."

Myles snorted with a smile. "Buy him a flashlight and have done of it."

I sat back on a couple of old sacks, accepted the bottle back again. "He's pretty well tied to the old ways. Doesn't care so much for the new."

"Well, times are changing."

"They sure are that."

Sitting there with nothing between the darkness and us but a flashlight and a bottle, I couldn't help thinking that nothing changed much about Myles. Give him a bottle of rum, gas for his truck, and work to stay away from, and he was happy. Of course he fished hard all summer. Often, he helped out old Claude MacRae the same way as I did Chester Gordon. Through the winter he mended nets for the old guy, speared the odd crate of eels for him if needed. I made my usual offer: "We're loading a freight car of potatoes tomorrow," I said, "if you're looking for something to do."

Myles pushed his hand through the air in my direction, shook his head once each way. "Winter's my time of rest," he declared. "Besides, I wouldn't be caught dead working for old Gordon. Break my back for the sake of his profit? No way."

"He breaks even like everyone else," I countered.

"My God!" Myles responded with irony, "a company man."

"You've got to admit, he pays out a lot of wages on this shore."

"Not to this bird he doesn't."

It was our usual winter's topic: Chester, potato shipments, the world of work. Myles attacked and I defended. It was all good-natured fun though. Myles had as sweet a disposition as a fellow could ask for. It's just that, like most simple people, he had to get upset about something before he could think clearly about it. I thought that I was probably the same; thought that Myles seemed to have been my brother-in-law all my life.

A gust of wind sailed into the rafters, interrupted our silence. I wanted Myles to know what I was thinking, but didn't quite know how to put it. Finally, I said it straight. "Chester says that Shirley and I should take a trip out to B.C. in the spring. To see his place out there. Says he'll pay our train fare out and back."

"What does Shirley say?"

"Haven't told her yet."

"I doubt she'd want to go out there any more than I would."

His unselfconscious retort deflated me. I sagged inside with the knowledge that he was right. Didn't want to let on though. "Chester still talks about the place out there as if he just left it," I said with a neutral chuckle.

"He's a miserable old ass."

"Well," I continued, "it's just that he doesn't care for the cold weather all that much."

"Too many mild winters have softened him up."

"If he was twenty winters younger I'd hate to be the one to cross him."

Myles nodded, considered the bottle.

I filled the silence: "Chester told me one time about that first summer he headed out west. As he put it, 'not a nickel to his name nor a pot to piss in'. His first job was on a big farm out in Saskatchewan. Spent his first day on a binder, cut one round of a field of oats in the morning, another round in the afternoon. That's how big the field was. Told me they didn't even think in acreage out there. Said it was all sections and quarter sections of land as far as the eye could see."

"It's a wonder he didn't take over the place for them."

"Chester told me that a man has no idea how large this country really is until he has ridden across it on the railway."

"Most fellows don't care."

"I suppose," I answered. "But it's a wonder to see how the old guy lights up when he talks about B.C., and about the enormity of the land out there: the totem poles, the mountains—stuff we never get to see." The night wind sounded a hollow assent, and I added with a sigh, "I don't know but I wouldn't mind seeing Chester's place out there."

"You're getting to be as bad as he is," Myles observed.

"I doubt it."

"No, hell, you'll be travelling back and forth, here and there, mouthing off about the growing season and calling the Island down to the lowest just like the old boy."

"Can't you just imagine him on a night like tonight," I said.

Myles grinned. "He's up there in the dark, shivering in his cap and loving it."

To tell the truth, I felt a little cheap in making fun of Chester right then. Fact is, I wanted to go out west just as Chester had done, wanted to see the mountains and prairies. There, in the dark, I could imagine a Chester Gordon some ten years younger than I was now, setting out on his own with nothing but himself to rely on. Seemed incredibly daring to me. Back in the past, when Grandpa was still living and Father was young, I could imagine Chester writing back to the folks about all he had seen, about what he was up to. I pictured again the photocard he had sent back from the Rocky Mountains. There was a picture of him on top of a mountain peak, and the caption read: "On Top of the World." On the back of the card he wrote that he was eating well and reading the Bible on Sundays.

He used to come home each summer and spend some time with Wilfred in fixing up the old Gordon homestead. Would stay just long enough to tire everyone of his descriptions of the "promised land" out west. He wore hats like the movie stars did, and was the first man around that I ever saw smoking factory made cigarettes. As a boy, I thought he must be pretty important by the way everybody talked about him. But it usually wasn't in the best of terms. I can still remember Loman Campbell spitting out between tobacco jets: "If it's so great out there, and so backward back here, why the hell doesn't he just stay out there." Wilfred and Father would always stand up for Chester though. I know they felt the same way as Loman Campbell did, but they would always say that Chester still felt at home on the Island, still loved to come back in the summers, but was a little resentful because no one ever went out west to visit him.

"I guess they used to call him 'the explorer'," I said to the silence of the old house.

"You keep talking about taking trips, and they'll be calling you the same thing," Myles answered.

"It wouldn't kill a fellow to see something a little different."

"But that's just it," Myles returned, "there *is* no difference. People, places, the land—it's all the same. Anything you or I want can be had right here."

Myles was right. There was no arguing with him. But his assurances gnawed me just the same. His shortsightedness was demeaning, and I knew I'd hear the same response from Shirley if I ever broached the topic of travelling out west. Myles and Shirley were too much alike, I thought. But Shirley was mine and I was Shirley's. Sort of cancelled things out and left us in one place. This rationalizing arithmetic ran in my head as I began to search for the kerosene lamps again. Sensing victory for his point of view, Myles held his bottle aloft to the darkness: "A fellow needn't travel any farther than he has to. Stay in one place and get some drinking done."

Spoken like a true nobody, I thought, but never let on a word. Who was I to be so important? Biting the inside of my cheek, I took the two lamps down from a shelf over the window, ran a finger over the layer of dust that covered them. Something abut their immobility struck me, and I looked beyond them out the window. I noticed the candle across the way had moved back to the bedroom. I wished I had never got out of that bed.

Both lamps lit easily. There was plenty of oil in each of them. I watched the lights against each other as they flickered soft and inconstant. I named them Father and Chester, and thought to myself that every place was a "promised land" to somebody in this world's endless geography of places. Indifference lifted my dissatisfaction and carried it across the ice-bound shore fields to the old cemetary by the church. Father's grave, Grandpa's grave, Chester's plot marked out right alongside Wilfred's, the good earth.

"Use the homestead like it's your own," Chester told me once. He laid his hand right on my shoulder and winked when he said it. Once, when I was a boy, he had placed that same hand on my shoulder in front of Father and the others, called me a "good worker." I thought it the highest praise possible. But then I remembered Shirley the first time she said that she loved me. I wished I hadn't said anything to Myles about travelling out west; wished I didn't have to carry these kerosene lamps back through the snowdrifts to Chester Gordon's place. Thought that I might as well check the temperature in the warehouse while I was back there.

My thoughts were stopped in their traces, however, as Myles punched me in the arm and pointed out the window. Sure enough, the power was back on. "Wouldn't you know it," I said, as we stood in the doorway and looked over at the place, at all the houses along the shore road. I felt a sullen desolate familiarity with it all. Looking back toward the Gordon homestead right then, it seemed to be lit up brighter than I had ever noticed before, and I felt a catch in my throat because for a second the homestead looked like it was on fire. I took a deep breath and cursed my own empty fears as we started toward the house.

I carried the lamps and gritted my teeth against the wind. Myles followed directly behind me, hummed a tune to himself as we tramped onto the porch. Shirley was at the door, and I heard Myles inquire as to what was on for dinner. It was his usual greeting.

But Shirley never answered, just turned off the radio as we came in, moved into the kitchen to pour tea. I followed. Told Shirley that I was going right over to the homestead, was going to put Chester to bed, and would have my tea as soon as I came back.

Shirley held my hand, said that she had been on the phone to Chester when the power came back on. He told her he had heard that the weather was not to blame for the power loss; that someone had run into a power pole over on the MacMurdo Road. Power had been knocked out along the shore.

Of course. Chester would be getting to the bottom of the matter. He'd be propped up on his day bed, dialing government numbers like an executive. His directories would be piled by his side. He would be demanding answers. No doubt he'd want to discuss it all with me. It would be a while before he would calm down enough to go to bed. Probably I'd have to drive him over in the morning to have a look at the scene of the accident. That is, if the roads were clear.

I didn't relish going out again tonight, but knew that I had to. I held Shirley close, felt her small, tight body, felt that all my discoveries were made. We had promised things to each other beyond what anyone could know, beyond any answers worth giving, beyond any place worth travelling to. The folds of her gown and her long loose hair hung suspended, and I pulled them together to me, inside my heavy jacket against my chest. My chin rested atop her head. I told her everything would be all right.

"It was a big tractor trailer," she went on, as she pulled away from my grasp. "Chester heard the report on the radio. Said that the driver was killed, but that the name hadn't been released yet."

I let her go reluctantly, saw there were tears in her eyes. "And Christmas is a week from Tuesday too," she said as she carried the kerosene lamps into the kitchen to wash them.

Biography

Rick Bowers was born on Prince Edward Island in 1955. He grew up on various air force bases in Canada and Europe, as well as on his grandfather's farm in Roxbury, P.E.I. He graduated from Summerside High School into the federal civil service, and from Dalhousie University into graduate school. He has been in and out of the academy ever since on scholarships from the Social Sciences and Humanities Research Council of Canada and from the Izaak Walton Killam Memorial Trust.

Bibliography

— "Yesterday and Forever," *The New Quarterly*, 3 (Spring 1983), 37-42.
— "Shelfoon," *The Antigonish Review*, No. 57 (Spring 1984), 19-23.
— "The Return Man," *The Pottersfield Portfolio*, 7 (1985-86), 10-14.

The Artist

Aré Gjesdal was born in Aalgaard, Norway in 1952. He studied art in Norway and Alberta. He is a boatbuilder and sailor who now lives on Devil's Island in Halifax Harbour with his wife, Dyane.